RUDDER GRANGE

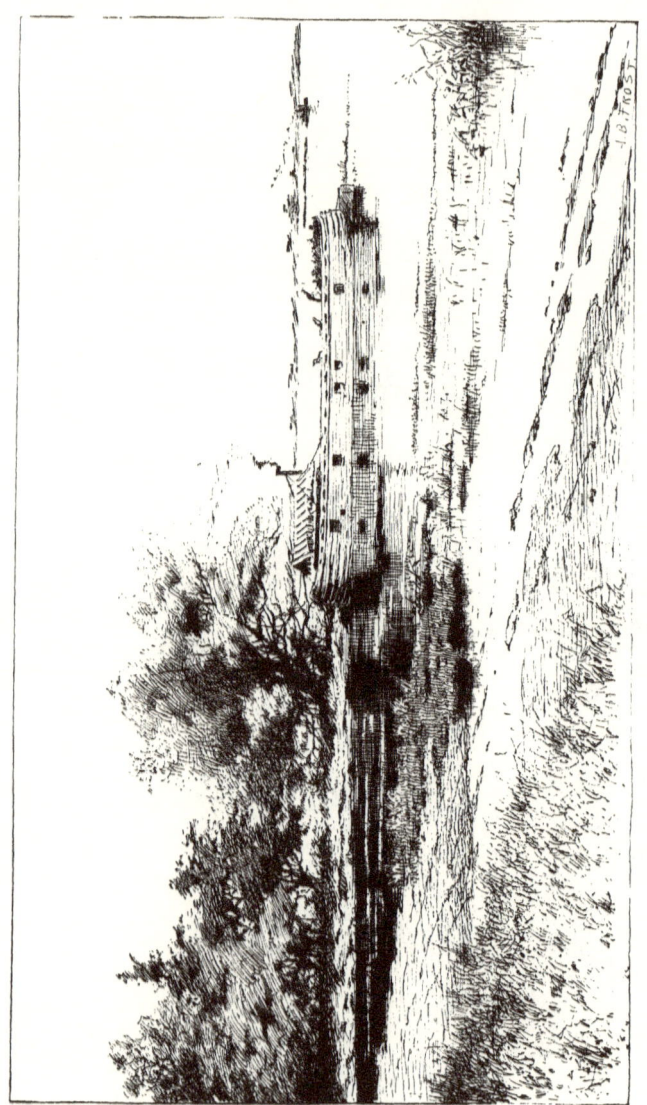

Rudder Grange.

RUDDER GRANGE

BY

FRANK R. STOCKTON

ILLUSTRATED

WILDSIDE PRESS

CONTENTS

CHAPTER   PAGE

I TREATING OF A NOVEL STYLE OF DWELL-
ING HOUSE 3

II TREATING OF A NOVEL STYLE OF
BOARDER 19

III TREATING OF A NOVEL STYLE OF GIRL 27

IV TREATING OF A NOVEL STYLE OF BURG-
LAR. 38

V POMONA PRODUCES A PARTIAL REVOLU-
TION IN RUDDER GRANGE . . 49

VI THE NEW RUDDER GRANGE . . . 58

VII TREATING OF AN UNSUCCESSFUL BROKER
AND A DOG 72

VIII POMONA ONCE MORE 83

IX WE CAMP OUT 93

X WET BLANKETS 108

XI THE BOARDER'S VISIT . . . 118

XII LORD EDWARD AND THE TREE-MAN . 131

XIII POMONA'S NOVEL 146

XIV POMONA TAKES A BRIDAL TRIP . . 164

XV IN WHICH TWO NEW FRIENDS DISPORT
THEMSELVES 175

v

CONTENTS

CHAPTER   PAGE

XVI In which an Old Friend Appears and
the Bridal Trip Takes a Fresh
Start 189

XVII In which We Take a Vacation and
Look for David Dutton . . 199

XVIII Our Tavern 210

XIX The Baby at Rudder Grange . 226

XX The Other Baby at Rudder Grange 235

ILLUSTRATIONS

Rudder Grange . . . . *Frontispiece*

FACING
PAGE

"My sudden entrance startled them" 24

"Mrs. Blaine" 32

"'Foiled again,' muttered the marsh-man" . . 84

"Give him the butt! Give him the butt!" . . 100

"These people have entered into a conspiracy
against us" 122

I looked up at the man 136

"Take that dog off of there!" 156

"'Hello!' 'Look a-there!'" 182

"They're tweens" 232

RUDDER GRANGE

RUDDER GRANGE

CHAPTER I

TREATING OF A NOVEL STYLE OF DWELLING-HOUSE

FOR some months after our marriage, Euphemia and I boarded. But we did not like it; indeed, there was no reason why we should. Euphemia said that she never felt at home except when she was out, which feeling, indicating such an excessively un-philosophic state of mind, was enough to make me desire to have a home of my own, where, except upon rare and exceptional occasions, my wife would never care to go out.

If you should want to rent a house, there are three ordinary ways to find one. One way is to advertise; another is to read the advertisements of other people, and a third method is to apply to a real-estate agent. But none of these plans is worth anything. The proper way is to know some one who will tell you of a house that will exactly suit you. Euphemia and I thoroughly investigated this matter, and I know that what I say is a fact.

We tried all the plans. When we advertised, we had about a dozen admirable answers, but in these, although everything seemed to suit, the amount of rent was not named. None of those in which the rent was named would do at all, and when I went to see the owners or agents of the suitable houses, they asked much higher rents than those mentioned in the unavailable answers—and this notwithstanding the fact that they always asserted that their terms were either very reasonable or else greatly reduced on account of the season being advanced—it was now the 15th of May.

Euphemia and I once wrote a book,—this was just before we were married,—in which we told young married people how to go to housekeeping and how much it would cost them. We knew all about it, for we had asked several people. Now, the prices demanded as yearly rental for furnished houses, by the owners and agents of whom I have been speaking, were, in some cases, more than we had stated a house could be bought and furnished for!

The advertisements of other people did not serve any better. There was always something wrong about the houses when we made close inquiries, and the trouble was generally in regard to the rent. With agents we had little better fortune. Euphemia sometimes went with me on my expeditions to real-estate offices, and she remarked that these offices were always in the basement, or else you had to go up to them in an elevator. There was nothing between these extremes, and it was a good deal the same way, she said, with their houses. They were all very low indeed in price and quality, or else too high.

One trouble was that we wanted a house in a country place, not very far from the city, and not very far

4

from the railroad-station or steamboat-landing. We also wanted the house to be nicely shaded and fully furnished, and not to be in a malarial neighborhood, or one infested by mosquitoes.

"If we do go to housekeeping," said Euphemia, "we might as well get a house to suit us, while we are about it. Moving is more expensive than a fire."

There was one man who offered us a house that almost suited us. It was near the water, had rooms enough, with some, but not very much, ground, and was very accessible to the city. The rent, too, was quite reasonable. But the house was unfurnished. The agent, however, did not think that this should present any obstacle to our taking it. He was sure that the owner would furnish it if we paid him ten per cent. on the value of the furniture he put into it. We agreed that if the landlord would do this, and let us furnish the house according to the plans laid down in our book, we would take the house. But unfortunately this arrangement did not suit the landlord, although he was in the habit of furnishing houses for tenants and charging them ten per cent. on the cost. I saw him myself and talked to him about it.

"But you see," said he, when I had shown him our list of articles necessary for the furnishing of a house, "it would not pay me to buy all these things and rent them out to you. If you only wanted heavy furniture, which would last for years, the plan would answer ; but you want everything. I believe the small conveniences you have on this list come to more money than the furniture and carpets."

"Oh, yes," said I. "We are not so very particular

5

about furniture and carpets, but these little conveniences are the things that make housekeeping pleasant and—speaking from a common-sense point of view—profitable."

"That may be," he answered, "but I can't afford to make matters pleasant and profitable for you in that way. Now, then, let us look at one or two particulars. Here on your list is an ice-pick, twenty-five cents. Now, if I buy that ice-pick and rent it to you at two and a half cents a year, I shall not get my money back unless it lasts you ten years. And even then, as it is not probable that I can sell that ice-pick after you have used it for ten years, I shall have made nothing at all by my bargain. And there are other things in that list, such as feather dusters and lamp-chimneys, that couldn't possibly last ten years. Don't you see my position?"

I saw it. We did not get that furnished house. Euphemia was greatly disappointed.

"It would have been just splendid," she said, "to have taken our book and to have ordered all these things at the stores, one after another, without even being obliged to ask the price."

I had my private doubts in regard to this matter of price. I was afraid that Euphemia generally set down the lowest prices and the best things. She did not mean to mislead, and her plan certainly made our book attractive. But it did not work very well in practice. We have a friend who undertook to furnish her house by our book, and she never could get the things as cheap as we had them quoted.

"But you see," said Euphemia to her, "we had to put them down at very low prices, because the model

house we speak of in the book is to be entirely furnished for just so much."

But, in spite of this explanation, our friend was not
satisfied.

We found ourselves obliged to give up the idea of
a furnished house. We would have taken an unfurnished one and furnished it ourselves, but we had not
money enough. We were dreadfully afraid that we
should have to continue to board.

It was now getting on toward summer,—at least, there
was only a part of a month of spring left,—and whenever I could get off from my business Euphemia and
I made little excursions into the country round about
the city. One afternoon we went up the river, and
there we saw a sight that transfixed us, as it were. On
the bank, a mile or so above the city, stood a canal-
boat. I say stood, because it was so firmly embedded
in the ground by the riverside that it would have
been almost as impossible to move it as to have turned
the Sphinx around. This boat, we soon found, was inhabited by an oysterman and his family. They had
lived there for many years, and were really doing
quite well. The boat was divided, inside, into rooms,
and these were papered and painted and nicely furnished. There was a kitchen, a living-room, a parlor,
and bedrooms. There were all sorts of conveniences,
carpets on the floors, pictures, and everything—at
least, so it seemed to us—to make a home comfortable.
This was not all done at once, the oysterman told me.
They had lived there for years, and had gradually
added this and that until the place was as we saw it.
He had an oyster-bed out in the river, and he made
cider in the winter, but where he got the apples I

don't know. There was really no reason why he should not get rich in time.

We went all over that house, and we praised everything so much that the oysterman's wife was delighted, and when we had some stewed oysters afterward,—eating them at a little table under a tree near by,—I believe she picked out the very largest oysters she had to stew for us. When we had finished our supper and had paid for it, and were going down to take our little boat again,—for we had rowed up the river,—Euphemia stopped and looked around her. Then she clasped her hands and exclaimed in an ecstatic undertone :

"We must have a canal-boat!"

And she never swerved from that determination.

After I had seriously thought over the matter, I could see no good reason against adopting this plan. It would certainly be a cheap method of living, and it would really be housekeeping. I grew more and more in favor of it. After what the oysterman had done, what might not we do? *He* had never written a book on housekeeping, nor, in all probability, had he considered the matter philosophically for one moment in all his life.

But it was not an easy thing to find a canal-boat. There were none advertised for rent—at least, not for housekeeping purposes.

We made many inquiries and took many a long walk along the water-courses in the vicinity of the city, but all in vain. Of course we talked a great deal about our project, and our friends became greatly interested in it, and of course, too, they gave us a great deal of advice, but we didn't mind that; we

RUDDER GRANGE

were philosophical enough to know that one cannot have fish without bones. They were good friends, and by being careful in regard to the advice, it did not interfere with our comfort.

We were beginning to be discouraged—at least, Euphemia was. Her discouragement is like water-cress: it generally comes up in a very short time after she sows her wishes. But then it withers away rapidly, which is a comfort. One evening we were sitting, rather disconsolately, in our room, and I was reading out the advertisements of country board in a newspaper, when in rushed Dr. Heare—one of our old friends. He was so full of something that he had to say that he didn't even ask us how we were. In fact, he didn't appear to want to know.

"I tell you what it is," said he, "I have found just the very thing you want."

"A canal-boat?" I cried.

"Yes," said he, "a canal-boat."

"Furnished?" asked Euphemia, her eyes glistening.

"Well, no," answered the doctor. "I don't think you could expect that."

"But we can't live on the bare floor," said Euphemia; "our house *must* be furnished."

"Well, then, I suppose this won't do," said the doctor, ruefully, "for there isn't so much as a boot-jack in it. It has most things that are necessary for a boat, but it hasn't anything that you could call house furniture; but dear me! I should think you could furnish it very cheaply and comfortably out of your book."

"Very true," said Euphemia, "if we could pick out the cheapest things, and then get some folks to buy a lot of the books."

"We could begin with very little," said I, trying hard to keep calm.

"Certainly," said the doctor, "you need make no more rooms, at first, than you could furnish."

"Then there are no rooms," said Euphemia.

"No; there is nothing but one vast apartment extending from stem to stern."

"Won't it be glorious!" said Euphemia to me. "We can first make a kitchen, and then a dining-room, and a bedroom, and then a parlor—just in the order in which our book says they ought to be furnished."

"Glorious!" I cried, no longer able to contain my enthusiasm. "I should think so. Doctor, where is this canal-boat?"

The doctor then went into a detailed statement.

The boat was stranded on the shore of the Scoldsbury River, not far below Ginx's. We knew where Ginx's was, because we had spent a very happy day there during our honeymoon.

The boat was a good one, but superannuated. That, however, would not interfere with its usefulness as a dwelling. We could get it—the doctor had seen the owner—for a small rental, and there was positively no end to its capabilities.

We sat up until twenty minutes past two, talking about that house. We ceased to call it a boat at about a quarter of eleven.

The next day I rented the boat and paid for a month in advance. Three days afterward we moved into it.

We had not much to move, which was a comfort, looking at it from one point of view. A carpenter had put up two partitions in the boat, which made three rooms—a kitchen, a dining-room, and a very long bedroom, which was to be cut up into a parlor, study, spare room, etc., as soon as circumstances should allow or my salary should be raised. Originally, all the doors and windows were in the roof, so to speak ; but our landlord allowed us to make as many windows to the side of the boat as we pleased, provided we gave him the wood we cut out. It saved him trouble, he said, but I did not understand him at the time. Accordingly, the carpenter made several windows for us, and put in sashes, which opened on hinges like the hasps of a trunk. Although our furniture did not amount to much at first, the very thought of living in this independent, romantic way was so delightful, Euphemia said, that furniture seemed a mere secondary matter.

We were obliged, indeed, to give up the idea of following the plan detailed in our book, because we had not the sum upon which the furnishing of a small house was therein based.

"And if we haven't the money," remarked Euphemia, "it would be of no earthly use to look at the book. It would only make us doubt our own calculations. You might as well try to make brick without mortar, as the children of Israel did."

"I could do that myself, my dear," said I, "but we won't discuss that subject now. We will buy just what we absolutely need, and then work up from that."

Acting on this plan, we bought first a small stove, because Euphemia said that we could sleep on the floor, if it were necessary, but we could not make a fire on the floor—at least, not often. Then we got a table and two chairs. The next thing we purchased was some hanging shelves for our books, and then Euphemia suddenly remembered the kitchen things. These, which were few, with some crockery, nearly brought us to the end of our resources; but we had enough for a big easy-chair which Euphemia was determined I should have, because I really needed it when I came home at night, tired with my long day's work at the office. I had always been used to an easy-chair, and it was one of her most delightful dreams to see me in a really nice one, comfortably smoking my pipe in my own house, after eating my own delicious little supper in company with my own dear wife. We selected the chair, and were about to order the things sent out to our future home, when I happened to think that we had no bed. I called Euphemia's attention to the fact.

She was thunderstruck.

"I never thought of that," she said. "We shall have to give up the stove."

"Not at all," said I, "we can't do that. We must give up the easy-chair."

"Oh, that would be too bad," said she. "The house would seem like nothing to me without the chair!"

"But we must do without it, my dear," said I, "at least, for a while. I can sit out on deck and smoke of an evening, you know."

"Yes," said Euphemia. "You can sit on the bulwarks, and I can sit by you. That will do very well. I'm sure I'm glad the boat has bulwarks."

So we resigned the easy-chair and bought a bedstead and some very plain bedding. The bedstead was what is sometimes called a "scissors-bed." We could shut it up when we did not want to sleep in it, and stand it against the wall.

When we packed up our trunks and left the boarding-house Euphemia fairly skipped with joy.

We went down to Ginx's in the first boat, having arranged that our furniture should be sent to us in the afternoon. We wanted to be there to receive it. The trip was wildly delirious. The air was charming, the sun was bright, and I had a whole holiday. When we reached Ginx's we found that the best way to get our trunks and ourselves to our house was to take a carriage, and so we took one. I told the driver to drive along the river road and I would tell him where to stop.

When we reached our boat, and had alighted, I said to the driver :

"You can just put our trunks inside, anywhere."

The man looked at the trunks and then looked at the boat. Afterward he looked at me.

"That boat ain't goin' anywhere," said he.

"I should think not," said Euphemia. "We shouldn't want to live in it if it were."

"You are going to live in it ?" said the man.

"Yes," said Euphemia.

"Oh !" said the man, and he took our trunks on board without another word.

It was not very easy for him to get the trunks into our new home. In fact, it was not easy for us to get there ourselves. There was a gang-plank with a rail on one side of it, which inclined from the shore to the deck of the boat at an angle of forty-five degrees ; and when the man had staggered up this plank with the trunks,—Euphemia said I ought to have helped him, but I really thought that it would be better for one person to fall off the plank than for two to go over together,—and we had paid him, and he had driven away in a speechless condition, we scrambled up and stood upon the threshold, or rather the after-deck, of our home.

It was a proud moment. Euphemia glanced around, her eyes full of happy tears, and then she took my arm and we went down-stairs; at least, we tried to go down in that fashion, but we soon found it necessary to go one at a time. We wandered over the whole extent of our mansion, and found that our carpenter had done his work better than the woman whom we had engaged to scrub and clean the house. Something akin to despair must have seized upon Euphemia, for she declared that the floors looked dirtier than on the occasion of her first visit, when we rented the boat.

But that did not discourage us. We felt sure that we would get it clean in time.

Early in the afternoon our furniture arrived, together with the other things we had bought, and the men who brought them over from the steamboat-landing had the brightest, merriest faces I ever noticed among that class of people. Euphemia said it was an excellent omen to have such cheerful fellows come to us on the very first day of our housekeeping.

Then we went to work. I put up the stove, which was not much trouble, as there was a place all ready in the deck for the stovepipe to be run through. Euphemia was somewhat surprised at the absence of a chimney, but I assured her that boats were very seldom built with chimneys. My dear little wife bustled about and arranged the pots and kettles on

14

nails that I drove into the kitchen walls. Then she made the bed in the bedroom, and I hung up a looking-glass and a few little pictures we had brought in our trunks.

Before four o'clock our house was in order. Then we began to be very hungry.

"My dear," said Euphemia, "we ought to have thought to bring something to cook."

"That is very true," said I, "but I think perhaps we would better walk up to Ginx's and get our supper to-night. You see, we are so tired and hungry."

"What!" cried Euphemia, "go to a hotel the very first day? I think it would be dreadful! Why, I have been looking forward to this first meal with the greatest delight. You can go up to the little store by the hotel and buy some things, and I will cook them, and we will have our first dear little meal here all alone by ourselves, at our own table and in our own house."

So this was determined upon, and after a hasty counting of the fund I had reserved for moving and kindred expenses, which had been sorely depleted during the day, I set out, and in about an hour returned with my first marketing.

I made a fire, using a lot of chips and blocks the carpenter had left, and Euphemia cooked the supper, and we ate it from our little table, with two large towels for a table-cloth.

It was the most delightful meal I ever ate!

And when we had finished, Euphemia washed the dishes,—the thoughtful creature had put some water on the stove to heat for the purpose while we were at supper,—and then we went on deck, or on the piazza, as Euphemia thought we would better call it, and there we had our smoke. I say *we*, for Euphemia always helps me to smoke by sitting by me, and she seems to enjoy it as much as I do.

When the shades of evening began to gather around us, I hauled in the gang-plank,—just like a delightful old drawbridge, Euphemia said,—although I hope, for the sake of our ancestors, that drawbridges were easier to haul in, and went to bed.

It is lucky we were tired and wanted to go to bed early, for we had forgotten all about lamps or candles.

For the next week we were two busy and happy people. I rose about half-past five and made the fire,—we found so much wood on the shore that I thought I should not have to add fuel to my expenses, —and Euphemia cooked the breakfast. I next went to a well belonging to a cottage near by where we had arranged for water privileges, and filled two buckets with delicious water and carried them home for Euphemia's use through the day. Then I hurried off to catch the train, for, as there was a station near Ginx's, I ceased to patronize the steamboat, the hours of which were not convenient. After a day of work and pleasurable anticipation at the office, I hastened back to my home, generally laden with a basket of provisions and various household necessities. Milk was brought to us daily from the above-mentioned cottage by a little toddler who seemed just able to carry the small tin bucket which held a lacteal pint. If the urchin had been the child of rich parents, as Euphemia sometimes observed, he would have been in his nurse's arms ; but, being poor, he was scarcely weaned before he began to carry milk around to other people.

RUDDER GRANGE

After I reached home came supper and the delightful evening hours, when over my pipe—I had given up cigars as being too expensive and inappropriate, and had taken to a tall pipe and canaster tobacco—we talked and planned, and told each other our day's experiences.

One of our earliest subjects of discussion was the name of our homestead. Euphemia insisted that it should have a name. I was quite willing, but we found it no easy matter to select an appropriate title.

I proposed a number of appellations intended to suggest the character of our home. Among these were "Safe Ashore," "Firmly Grounded," and some other names of that style, but Euphemia did not fancy any of them. She wanted a suitable name, of course, she said, but it must be something that would *sound* like a house and *be* like a boat.

"Partitionville" she objected to, and "Gangplank Terrace" did not suit her because it suggested convicts going out to work, which naturally was unpleasant.

At last, after days of talk and cogitation, we named our house "Rudder Grange."

To be sure, it was not exactly a grange; but then, it had such an enormous rudder that the justice of this part of the title seemed to overbalance any little inaccuracy in the other portion.

But we did not spend all our spare time in talking. An hour or two every evening was occupied in what we called "fixing the house," and gradually the inside of our abode began to look like a conventional dwelling. We put matting on the floors, and cheap but very pretty paper on the walls. We added now a

17

couple of chairs, and now a table or something for the kitchen. Frequently, especially of a Sunday, we had company, and our guests were always charmed with Euphemia's cunning little meals. The dear girl loved good eating so much that she could scarcely fail to be a good cook.

We worked hard, and were very happy. And thus the weeks passed on.

CHAPTER II

In this delightful way of living only one thing troubled us. We did not save any money. There were so many little things that we wanted, and so many little things that were so cheap, that I spent pretty much all I made, which was far from the philosophical plan of living I wished to follow.

We talked this matter over a great deal after we had lived in our new home for about a month, and we came at last to the conclusion that we would take a boarder.

We had no trouble in getting a boarder, for we had a friend, a young man engaged in the flour business, who was very anxious to come and live with us. He had been to see us two or three times, and had expressed himself charmed with our household arrangements.

So we made terms with him. The carpenter partitioned off another room, and our boarder brought his trunk and a large red velvet arm-chair, and took up his abode at Rudder Grange.

We liked our boarder very much, but he had some peculiarities. I suppose everybody has them. Among other things, he was very fond of telling us what we

19

ought to do. He suggested more improvements in the first three days of his sojourn with us than I had thought of since we commenced housekeeping; and what made the matter worse, his suggestions were generally very good ones. Had it been otherwise I might have borne his remarks more complacently; but to be continually told what you ought to do, and to know that you ought to do it, is extremely annoying.

He was very anxious that I should take off the rudder, which was certainly useless to a boat situated as ours was, and make an ironing-table of it. I persisted that the laws of symmetrical propriety required that the rudder should remain where it was—that the very name of our home would be interfered with by its removal; but he insisted that "Ironing-Table Grange" would be just as good a name, and that symmetrical propriety in such a case did not amount to a row of pins.

The result was that we had the ironing-table, and that Euphemia was very much pleased with it. A great many other improvements were projected and carried out by him, and I was very much worried. He made a flower-garden for Euphemia on the extreme forward deck, and having borrowed a wheelbarrow, he wheeled dozens of loads of arable dirt up our gang-plank and dumped them out on the deck. When he had covered the garden with a suitable depth of earth, he smoothed it off and then planted flower-seeds. It was rather late in the season, but most of them came up. I was pleased with the garden, but sorry I had not made it myself.

One afternoon I got away from the office considerably earlier than usual, and I hurried home to enjoy the short period of daylight that I would have before supper. It had been raining the day before, and as the bottom of our garden leaked so that earthy water trickled down at one end of our bedroom, I intended to devote a short time to stuffing up the cracks in the ceiling or bottom of the deck—whichever seems the most appropriate.

But when I reached a bend in the river road whence I always had the earliest view of my establishment, I did not have that view. I hurried on. The nearer I approached the place where I lived, the more horror-stricken I became. There was no mistaking the fact.

The boat was not there!

In an instant the truth flashed upon me.

The water was very high—the rain had swollen the river—my house had floated away!

It was Wednesday. On Wednesday afternoons our boarder came home early.

I clapped my hat tightly on my head and ground my teeth.

"Confound that boarder!" I thought. "He has been fooling with the anchor. He always said it was of no use, and he has taken advantage of my absence, hauled it up, and has floated away, and has gone—gone with my wife and my home!"

Euphemia and Rudder Grange had gone off together,—where I knew not,—and with them that horrible suggester!

I ran wildly along the bank. I called aloud. I shouted and hailed each passing craft,—of which there were only two,—but their crews must have been very inattentive to the woes of landsmen, or else they did not hear me, for they paid no attention to my cries.

RUDDER GRANGE

I met a fellow with an axe on his shoulder, and I shouted to him before I reached him:

"Hello! did you see a boat—a house, I mean—floating up the river?"

"A boat-house?" asked the man.

"No, a house-boat," I gasped.

"Didn't see nothin' like it," said the man, and he passed on, to his wife and home, no doubt. But me! Oh, where was my wife and my home?

I met several people, but none of them had seen a fugitive canal-boat.

How many thoughts came into my brain as I ran along that river road! If that wretched boarder had not taken the rudder for an ironing-table he might have steered inshore! Again and again I confounded —as far as mental ejaculations could do it—his suggestions.

I was rapidly becoming frantic when I met a person who hailed me.

"Hello!" he said, "are you after a canal-boat adrift?"

"Yes," I panted.

"I thought you was," he said. "You looked that way. Well, I can tell you where she is. She's stuck fast in the reeds at the lower end o' Peter's P'int."

"Where's that?" said I.

"Oh, it's about a mile furder up. I seed her a-driftin' up with the tide,—big flood-tide to-day,—and I thought I'd see somebody after her afore long. Anything aboard?"

Anything!

I could not answer the man. Anything, indeed! I hurried up the river without a word. Was the

22

boat a wreck? I scarcely dared to think of it. I scarcely dared to think at all.

The man called after me, and I stopped. I could but stop, no matter what I might hear.

"Hello, mister," he said, "got any tobacco?"

I walked up to him. I took hold of him by the lapel of his coat. It was a dirty lapel, as I remember even now, but I did not mind that.

"Look here," said I. "Tell me the truth; I can bear it. Was that vessel wrecked?"

The man looked at me a little queerly. I could not exactly interpret his expression.

"You're sure you kin bear it?" said he.

"Yes," said I, my hand trembling as I held his coat.

"Well, then," said he, "it's more'n I kin," and he jerked his coat out of my hand, and sprang away. When he reached the other side of the road, he turned and shouted at me as though I had been deaf.

"Do you know what I think?" he yelled. "I think you're a darned lunatic;" and with that he went his way.

I hastened on to Peter's Point. Long before I reached it I saw the boat.

It was apparently deserted; but still I pressed on. I must know the worst. When I reached the Point, I found that the boat had run aground, with her head in among the long reeds and mud, and the rest of her hull lying at an angle from the shore.

There was consequently no way for me to get on board but to wade through the mud and reeds to her bow, and then climb up as well as I could.

This I did, but it was not easy. Twice I sank above my knees in mud and water, and had it not been for reeds, masses of which I frequently clutched when I thought I was going over, I believe I should have fallen down and come to my death in that horrible marsh. When I reached the boat, I stood up to my hips in water, and saw no way of climbing up. The gang-plank had undoubtedly floated away, but even if it had not, it would have been of no use to me in my position.

I was desperate. I clasped the post that they put in the bow of canal-boats; I stuck my toes and my finger-nails in the cracks between the boards,—how glad I was that the boat was an old one and had cracks!—and so, painfully and slowly, slipping part way down once or twice, and besliming myself from chin to foot, I climbed up that post and scrambled upon deck. In an instant I reached the top of the stairs, and in another instant I rushed below.

There sat my wife and our boarder, one on each side of the dining-room table, complacently playing checkers!

My sudden entrance startled them. My appearance startled them still more.

Euphemia sprang to her feet and tottered toward me.

"Mercy!" she exclaimed. "Has anything happened?"

"Happened!" I gasped.

"Look here," cried the boarder, clutching me by the arm, "what a condition you're in! Did you fall in?"

"Fall in!" said I.

Euphemia and the boarder looked at each other. I looked at them. Then I opened my mouth in earnest.

"My sudden entrance startled them."

"I suppose you don't know," I yelled, "that you have drifted away!"

"By George!" cried the boarder, and in two bounds he was on deck.

Dirty as I was, Euphemia fell into my arms. I told her all. She had not known a bit of it!

The boat had so gently drifted off, and had so gently grounded among the reeds, that the voyage had never so much as disturbed their games of checkers.

"He plays such a splendid game," Euphemia sobbed, "and just as you came I thought I was going to beat him. I had two kings and two pieces on the next to last row, and you are nearly drowned! You'll get your death of cold—and—and he had only one king."

She led me away, and I undressed and washed myself and put on my Sunday clothes.

When I reappeared I went out on deck with Euphemia. The boarder was there, standing by the petunia-bed. His arms were folded and he was thinking profoundly. As we approached he turned toward us.

"You were right about that anchor," he said, "I should not have hauled it in. But it was such a little anchor that I thought it would be of more use on board as a garden hoe."

"A very little anchor will sometimes do very well," said I, cuttingly, "when it is hooked around a tree."

"Yes, there is something in that," said he.

It was now growing late, and as our agitation subsided we began to be hungry. Fortunately, we had everything necessary on board, and as it really did not make any difference in our household economy where we happened to be located, we had supper quite as usual. In fact, the kettle had been put on to boil during the checker-playing.

After supper we went on deck to smoke, as was our custom; but there was a certain coolness between me and our boarder.

Early the next morning I arose and went up-stairs to consider what would better be done, when I saw the boarder standing on shore, near by.

"Hello!" he cried, "the tide's down and I came ashore without any trouble. You stay where you are. I've hired a couple of mules to tow the boat back. They'll be here when the tide rises. And hello! I've found the gang-plank. It floated ashore about a quarter of a mile below here."

In the course of the afternoon the mules and two men with a long rope appeared, and we were then towed back where we belonged.

Our boarder remained with us, as the weather continued to be fine, and the coolness between us gradually diminished. But after that, the boat was moored at both ends, and twice a day I looked to see if the ropes were all right.

CHAPTER III

TREATING OF A NOVEL STYLE OF GIRL

ONE afternoon, as I was hurrying down Broadway to catch the five-o'clock train, I met Waterford. He is an old friend of mine, and I used to like him pretty well.

"Hello!" said he, "where are you going?"

"Home," I answered.

"Is that so?" said he. "I didn't know you had one."

I was a little nettled at this, and so I said, somewhat roughly, perhaps:

"But you must have known I lived somewhere."

"Oh, yes, but I thought you boarded," said he. "I had no idea that you had a home."

"But I have one, and a very pleasant home, too. You must excuse me for not stopping longer, as I must catch my train."

"Oh! I'll walk along with you," said Waterford, and so we went down the street together.

"Where is your little house?" he asked.

Why in the world he thought it was a little house I could not at the time imagine, unless he supposed that two people would not require a large one. But

I know, now, that he lived in a very little house himself.

But it was of no use getting angry with Waterford, especially as I saw he intended walking all the way down to the ferry with me, so I told him I did not live in any house at all.

"Why, where *do* you live?" he exclaimed, stopping short.

"I live in a boat," said I.

"A boat! A sort of 'Rob Roy' arrangement, I suppose. Well, I would not have thought that of you. And your wife, I suppose, has gone home to her people?"

"She has done nothing of the kind," I answered. "She lives with me, and she likes it very much. We are extremely comfortable, and our boat is not a canoe, or any such nonsensical affair. It is a large, commodious canal-boat."

Waterford turned around and looked at me.

"Are you a deck-hand?" he asked.

"Deck-grandmother!" I exclaimed.

"Well, you needn't get mad about it," he said. "I didn't mean to hurt your feelings; but I couldn't see what else you could be on a canal-boat. I don't suppose, for instance, that you're captain."

"But I am," said I.

"Look here!" said Waterford; "this is coming it rather strong, isn't it?"

As I saw he was getting angry, I told him all about it—how we had hired a stranded canal-boat and had fitted it up as a house, and how we lived so cosily in it, and had called it "Rudder Grange," and how we had taken a boarder.

"Well!" said he, "this certainly is surprising. I'm coming out to see you some day. It will be better than going to Barnum's."

I told him—it is the way of society—that we would be glad to see him, and we parted. Waterford never did come to see us, and I merely mention this incident to show how some of our friends talked about Rudder Grange when they first heard that we lived there.

After dinner that evening, when I went up on deck with Euphemia to have my smoke, we saw the boarder sitting on the bulwarks near the garden, with his legs dangling down outside.

"Look here!" said he.

I looked, but there was nothing unusual to see.

"What is it?" I asked.

He turned around and, seeing Euphemia, said: "Nothing."

It would be a very stupid person who could not take such a hint as that, and so, after a walk around the garden, Euphemia took occasion to go below to look at the kitchen fire.

As soon as she had gone, the boarder turned to me and said:

"I'll tell you what it is. She's working herself sick."

"Sick?" said I. "Nonsense!"

"No nonsense about it," he replied.

The truth was that the boarder was right and I was wrong. We had spent several months at Rudder Grange, and during this time Euphemia had been working very hard, and she really was beginning to look pale and thin. Indeed, it would be very wearying for any woman of culture and refinement, unused to housework, to cook and care for two men, and to do all the work of a canal-boat besides.

But I saw Euphemia so constantly, and thought so much of her, and had her image so continually in my heart, that I did not notice this until our boarder now called my attention to it. I was sorry that he had to do it.

"If I were in your place," said he, "I would get her a servant."

"If you were in my place," I replied, somewhat cuttingly, "you would probably suggest a lot of little things which would make everything very easy for her."

"I'd try to," he answered, without getting in the least angry.

Although I felt annoyed that he had suggested it, still I made up my mind that Euphemia must have a servant.

She agreed quite readily when I proposed the plan, and she urged me to go to see the carpenter that very day, and get him to come and partition off a little room for the girl.

It was some time, of course, before the room was made,—for who ever heard of a carpenter coming at the very time he was wanted?—and when it was finished, Euphemia occupied all her spare moments in getting it in nice order for the servant when she should come. I thought she was taking too much trouble, but she had her own ideas about such things.

"If a girl is lodged like a pig you must expect her to behave like a pig, and I don't want that kind."

So she put up pretty curtains at the girl's window, and with a box that she stood on end, and some old muslin and a lot of tacks, she made a toilet-table so neat and convenient that I thought she ought to take it into our room and give the servant our wash-stand.

But all this time we had no girl; and as I had made up my mind about the matter, I naturally grew impatient, and at last I determined to go and get a girl myself.

One day, at lunch-time, I went to an intelligence office in the city. There I found a large room on the second floor, and some ladies and one or two men sitting about, and a small room back of it crowded with girls from eighteen to sixty-eight years old. There were also girls upon the stairs, and girls in the hall below, besides some girls standing on the sidewalk before the door.

When I made known my business and had paid my fee, one of the several proprietors who were wandering about the front room went into the back apartment, and soon returned with a tall Irishwoman with a bony, weather-beaten face and a large weather-beaten shawl. This woman was told to take a chair by my side. Down sat the huge creature and stared at me. I did not feel very easy under her scrutinizing gaze, but I bore it as best I could, and immediately began to ask her all the appropriate questions I could think of. Some she answered satisfactorily, and some she did not answer at all; but as soon as I made a pause she began to put questions herself.

"How many servants do you kape?" she asked.

I answered that we intended to get along with one, and if she understood her business, I thought she would find her work very easy, and the place a good one.

RUDDER GRANGE

She turned sharply upon me and said:

"Have ye stationary wash-tubs?"

I hesitated. I knew our wash-tubs were not stationary, for I had helped to carry them about. But they might be screwed fast and made stationary, if that were an important object. But before making this answer I thought of the great conveniences for washing presented by our residence, surrounded as it was, at high tide, by water.

"Why, we live in a stationary wash-tub," I said, smiling.

The woman looked at me steadfastly for a minute, and then she rose to her feet. Then she called out, as if she were crying fish or strawberries:

"Mrs. Blaine!"

The female keeper of the intelligence office, and the male keeper, and a thin clerk, and all the women in the back room, and all the patrons in the front room, jumped up and gathered around us.

Astonished and somewhat disconcerted, I rose to my feet and confronted the tall Irishwoman, and stood smiling in an uncertain sort of a way, as if it were all very funny; but I could not see the point. I think I must have impressed the people with the idea that I wished I had not come.

"He says," exclaimed the woman, as if some other huckster were crying fish on the other side of the street—"he says he lives in a wash-toob."

"He's crazy!" ejaculated Mrs. Blaine, with an air that indicated "policeman" as plainly as if she had put her thought into words.

A low murmur ran through the crowd of women, while the thin clerk edged toward the door.

"Mrs. Blaine."

RUDDER GRANGE

I saw there was no time to lose. I stepped back a little from the tall savage, who was breathing like a hot-air engine in front of me, and made my explanations to the company. I told the tale of Rudder Grange, and showed them how it was like a stationary tionary wash-tub—at certain stages of the tide.

I was listened to with great attention. When I had finished the tall woman turned around and faced the assemblage.

"An' he wants a cook to make soup! In a canal-boat!" said she; and off she marched into the back room, followed closely by all the other women.

"I don't think we have any one here who would suit you," said Mrs. Blaine.

I did not think so, either. What on earth would Euphemia have done with that volcanic Irishwoman in her little kitchen! I took up my hat and bade Mrs. Blaine good morning.

"Good morning," said she, with a distressing smile.

She had one of those mouths that look exactly like a gash in the face.

I went home without a girl. In a day or two Euphemia went to town and got one. Apparently she got her without any trouble, but I am not sure.

She went to a "Home"—Saint Somebody's Home—a place where they keep orphans to let, so to speak, and here she selected a light-haired, medium-sized orphan, and brought her home.

The girl's name was Pomona. Whether or not her parents gave her this name is doubtful. At any rate, she did not seem quite decided in her mind about it herself, for she had not been with us more than two weeks before she expressed a desire to be called Clare.

33

This longing of her heart, however, was denied her, and Euphemia, who was always correct, called her Pomona. I did the same whenever I could think not to say Bologna—which seemed to come very pat, for some reason or other.

She was an earnest, hearty girl. She was always in a good humor, and when I asked her to do anything, she assented in a bright, cheerful way, and in a loud, hearty tone full of good-fellowship, as though she would say :

"Certainly, my high old cock ! To be sure I will. Don't worry about it—give your mind no more uneasiness on *that* subject. I'll bring you some hot water in two minutes."

She did not know very much, but she was delighted to learn, and she was very strong. Whatever Euphemia told her to do she did instantly with a bang. What pleased her better than anything else was to run up and down the gang-plank, carrying buckets of water to water the garden. She delighted in outdoor work, and sometimes dug so vigorously in our garden that she brought up pieces of the deck-planking with every shovelful.

Our boarder took the greatest interest in her, and sometimes watched her movements so intently that he let his pipe go out.

"What a whacking girl that would be to tread out grapes in the vineyards of Italy ! She'd make wine cheap," he once remarked.

"Then I'm glad she isn't there," said Euphemia, "for wine oughtn't to be cheap."

Euphemia was a thorough little temperance woman, and was always true to her principles.

RUDDER GRANGE

The one thing about Pomona that troubled me more than anything else was her taste for literature. It was not literature to which I objected, but her very peculiar taste. She would read in the kitchen every night after she had washed the dishes, but if she had not read aloud it would not have made so much difference to me. But I am naturally very sensitive to external impressions, and I do not like the company of people who, like our girl, cannot read without pronouncing in a measured and distinct voice every word of what they are reading. And when the matter thus read appeals to one's every sentiment of aversion, and there is no way of escaping it, the case is hard indeed.

From the first I felt inclined to order Pomona, if she could not attain the power of silent perusal, to cease from reading altogether; but Euphemia would not hear to this.

"Poor thing!" said she, "it would be cruel to take from her her only recreation. And she says she can't read any other way. You needn't listen if you don't want to."

This was all very well from an abstract point of view; but the fact was that, in practice, the more I did not want to listen, the more I heard.

As the evenings were often cool, we sat in our dining-room, and the partition between this room and the kitchen seemed to have no influence whatever in arresting sound. So that when I was trying to read or to reflect, it was by no means exhilarating to my mind to hear from the next room that:

"The La dy Ce sel i a now si zed the weep on and all though the boor ly vil ly an re tain ed his vy gor ous

35

hold she drew the blade through his fin gers and hoorl
ed it far be hind her dryp ping with jore."

This sort of thing, kept up for an hour or so at a
time, used to drive me nearly wild. But Euphemia
did not mind it. I believe that she had so delicate a
sense of what was proper that she did not hear Pomona's private readings.

On one occasion even Euphemia's influence could
scarcely restrain me from violent interference.

It was our boarder's night out, when he was de-
tained in town by his business, and Pomona was sitting up to let him in. This was necessary, for our
front door, or main-hatchway, had no night-latch,
but was fastened by means of a bolt. Euphemia and
I used to sit up for him, but that was earlier in the
season, when it was pleasant to be out on deck until
quite a late hour. But Pomona never objected to
sitting—or getting—up late, and so we allowed this
weekly duty to devolve on her.

On this particular night I was very tired and sleepy,
and soon after I got into bed I dropped into a delightful slumber. But it was not long before I was
awakened by the fact that:

"Sa rah did not fl inch but gras ped the heat ed i ron
in her un in jur ed hand and when the ra bid an i mal
a proach ed she thr ust the lur id po ker in his—"

"My conscience!" said I to Euphemia, "can't that
girl be stopped?"

"You wouldn't have her sit there and do nothing,
would you?" said she.

"No; but she needn't read out that way."

"She can't read any other way," said Euphemia
drowsily.

"Yell af ter yell res oun ded as he wil dly spr rang—"

"I can't stand that, and I won't," said I. "Why don't she go into the kitchen?—the dining-room's no place for her."

"She must not sit there," said Euphemia. "There's a window-pane out. Can't you cover up your head?"

"I shall not be able to breathe if I do; but I suppose that's no matter," I replied.

The reading continued:

"Ha, ha! Lord Mar mont thun der ed thou too shalt suf fer all that this poor—"

I sprang out of bed.

Euphemia thought I was going for my pistol, and she gave one bound and stuck her head out of the door.

"Pomona, fly!" she cried.

"Yes, sma'am," said Pomona; and she got up and flew—not very fast, I imagine. Where she flew to I don't know, but she took the lamp with her, and I could hear distant syllables of agony and blood, until the boarder came home and Pomona went to bed.

I think this made an impression upon Euphemia, for, although she did not speak to me upon the subject, or any other, that night, the next time I heard Pomona reading, the words ran somewhat thus:

"The as ton ish ing che ap ness of land is ac count ed for by the want of home mar kets, of good ro ads and che ap me ans of trans por ta ti on in ma ny sec ti ons of the State."

CHAPTER IV

TREATING OF A NOVEL STYLE OF BURGLAR

I HAVE spoken of my pistol. During the early part of our residence at Rudder Grange I never thought of such a thing as owning a pistol.

But it was different now. I kept a Colt's revolver loaded in the bureau-drawer in our bedroom.

The cause of this change was burglars. Not that any of these unpleasant persons had visited us, but we very much feared they would. Several houses in the vicinity had been entered during the past month, and we never could tell when our turn would come.

To be sure, our boarder suggested that if we were to anchor out a little farther at night, no burglar would risk catching his death of cold by swimming out to us; but Euphemia having replied that it would be rather difficult to move a canal-boat every night without paddle-wheels or sails or mules, especially if it were aground, this plan was considered to be effectually disposed of.

So we made up our minds that we must fasten up everything very securely, and I bought a pistol and two burglar-alarms. One of these I affixed to the most exposed window, and the other to the door which opened on the deck. These alarms were very simple

38

affairs, but they were good enough. When they were properly attached to a window or door, and it was opened, a little gong sounded like a violently deranged clock striking all the hours of the day at once.

The window did not trouble us much, but it was rather irksome to have to make the attachment to the door every night and to take it off every morning. However, as Euphemia said, it was better to take a little trouble than to have the house full of burglars, which was true enough.

We made all the necessary arrangements in case burglars should make an inroad upon us. At the first sound of the alarm, Euphemia and the girl were to lie flat on the floor or get under their beds. Then the boarder and I were to stand up back to back, each with pistol in hand, and fire away, revolving on a common centre the while. In this way, by aiming horizontally about four feet from the floor, we could rake the premises, and run no risk of shooting each other or the women of the family.

To be sure, there were some slight objections to this plan. The boarder's room was at some distance from ours, and he would probably not hear the alarm, and the burglars might not be willing to wait while I went forward and roused him up and brought him to our part of the house. But this was a minor difficulty. I had no doubt but that, if it should be necessary, I could manage to get our boarder into position in plenty of time.

It was not very long before there was an opportunity of testing the plan.

About twelve o'clock one night one of the alarms

—that on the kitchen window—went off with a whir and a wild succession of clangs. For a moment I thought the morning train had arrived, and then I woke up. Euphemia was already under the bed.

I hurried on a few clothes, and tried to find the bureau in the dark. This was not easy, as I lost my bearings entirely. But I found it at last, got the top drawer open, and took out my pistol. Then I slipped out of the room, hurried up the stairs, opened the door, setting off the alarm there, by the way, and ran along the deck (there was a cold night wind), and hastily descended the steep steps that led into the boarder's room. The door that was at the bottom of the steps was not fastened, and as I opened it a little stray moonlight illumed the room. I hastily stepped to the bed and shook the boarder by the shoulder. He kept *his* pistol under his pillow.

In an instant he was on his feet, his hand grasped my throat, and the cold muzzle of his Derringer pistol was at my forehead. It was an awfully big muzzle, like the mouth of a bottle.

I do not know when I lived so long as during the first minute that he held me thus.

"Rascal!" he said. "Do as much as breathe, and I'll pull the trigger."

I did not breathe.

I had an accident insurance on my life. Would it hold good in a case like this? Or would Euphemia have to go back to her father?

He pushed me back into the little patch of moonlight.

"Oh! is it you?" he said, relaxing his grasp. "What do you want? A mustard-plaster?"

He had a package of patent plasters in his room. You took one and dipped it in hot water, and it was all ready.

"No," said I, gasping a little. "Burglars."

"Oh!" he said, and he put down his pistol and put on his clothes.

"Come along," he said, and away we went over the deck.

When we reached the stairs all was dark and quiet below.

It was a matter of hesitancy as to going down.

I started to go down first, but the boarder held me back.

"Let me go down," he said.

"No," said I, "my wife is there."

"That's the very reason you should not go," he said. "She is safe enough yet, and they would fire only at a man. It would be a bad job for her if you were killed. I'll go down."

So he went down, slowly and cautiously, his pistol in one hand, and his life in the other, as it were.

When he reached the bottom of the steps I changed my mind. I could not remain above while the burglar and Euphemia were below, so I followed.

The boarder was standing in the middle of the dining-room, into which the stairs led. I could not see him, but I put my hand against him as I was feeling my way across the floor.

I whispered to him :

"Shall we put our backs together and revolve and fire?"

"No," he whispered back, "not now; he may be on a shelf by this time, or under a table. Let's look him up."

I confess that I was not very anxious to look him up, but I followed the boarder as he slowly made his way toward the kitchen door. As we opened the door we instinctively stopped.

The window was open, and by the light of the moon that shone in we saw the rascal standing on a chair, leaning out of the window, evidently just ready to escape. Fortunately, we were unheard.

Let's pull him in," whispered the boarder.

"No," I whispered in reply. "We don't want him in. Let's hoist him out."

"All right," returned the boarder.

We laid our pistols on the floor, and softly approached the window. Being barefooted, our steps were noiseless.

"Hoist when I count three," breathed the boarder into my ear.

We reached the chair. Each of us took hold of two of its legs.

"One—two—three!" said the boarder, and together we gave a tremendous lift and shot the wretch out of the window.

The tide was high, and there was a good deal of water around the boat. We heard a rousing splash outside.

Now there was no need of silence.

"Shall we run on deck and shoot him as he swims?" I cried.

"No," said the boarder, "we'll get the boat-hook, and jab him if he tries to climb up."

We rushed on deck. I seized the boat-hook and looked over the side. But I saw no one.

"He's gone to the bottom!" I exclaimed.

"He didn't go very far, then," said the boarder, "for it's not more than two feet deep there."

Just then our attention was attracted by a voice from the shore:

"Will you please let down the gang-plank?"

We looked ashore, and there stood Pomona, dripping from every pore.

We spoke no words, but lowered the gang-plank. She came aboard.

"Good night!" said the boarder, and he went to bed.

"Pomona!" said I, "what have you been doing?"

"I was a-lookin' at the moon, sir, when pop! the chair bounced, and out I went."

"You shouldn't do that," I said sternly. "Some day you'll be drowned. Take off your wet things and go to bed."

"Yes, sma'am—sir, I mean," said she, as she went down-stairs.

When I reached my room I lighted the lamp, and found Euphemia still under the bed.

"Is it all right?" she asked.

"Yes," I answered. "There was no burglar. Pomona fell out of the window."

"Did you get her a plaster?" asked Euphemia, drowsily.

"No, she did not need one. She's all right now. Were you worried about me, dear?"

"No; I trusted in you entirely, and I think I dozed a little under the bed."

In one minute she was asleep.

The boarder and I did not make this matter a subject of conversation afterward, but Euphemia gave the girl a lecture on her careless ways, and made her take several Dover's powders the next day.

An important fact in domestic economy was discovered about this time by Euphemia and myself. Perhaps we were not the first to discover it, but we certainly did find it out; and this fact was that housekeeping costs money. At the' end of every week we counted up our expenditures,—it was no trouble at all to count up our receipts,—and every week the result was more unsatisfactory.

"If we could only get rid of the disagreeable balance that has to be taken along all the time, and which gets bigger and bigger like a snowball, I think we would find the accounts more satisfactory," said Euphemia.

This was on a Saturday night. We always got our pencils and paper and money at the end of the week.'

"Yes," said I, with an attempt to appear facetious and unconcerned, "but it would be all well enough if we could take that snowball to the fire and melt it down."

"But there never is any fire where there are snowballs," said Euphemia.

"No," said I, "and that's just the trouble."

It was on the following Thursday, when I came home in the evening, that Euphemia met me with a glowing face. It rather surprised me to see her look so happy, for she had been very quiet and preoccupied for the first part of the week; so much so, indeed, that I had thought of ordering smaller roasts for a week or two, and taking her to a Thomas Concert with the money saved. But this evening she looked as if she did not need Thomas's orchestra.

"What makes you so bright, my dear?" said I, when I had greeted her. "Has anything jolly happened?"

"No," said she, "nothing yet; but I am going to make a fire to melt snowballs."

Of course I was very anxious to know how she was going to do it, but she would not tell me. It was a plan that she intended to keep to herself until she saw how it worked. I did not press her, because she had so few secrets, and I did not hear anything about this plan until it had been carried out.

Her scheme was as follows : After thinking over our financial condition and puzzling her brain to find out some way of bettering it, she had come to the conclusion that she would make some money by her own exertions to help defray our household expenses. She never had made any money, but that was no reason why she should not begin. It was too bad that I should have to toil and toil, and not make nearly enough money, after all. So she would go to work and earn something with her own hands.

She had heard of an establishment in the city where ladies of limited means, or transiently impecunious, could, in a very quiet and private way, get sewing to do. They could thus provide for their needs without any one but the officers of the institution knowing anything about it.

So Euphemia went to this place, and she got some work. It was not a very large bundle, but it was larger than she had been accustomed to carry, and, what was perfectly dreadful, it was wrapped up in a newspaper! When Euphemia told me the story, she said that this was too much for her courage. She

45

could not go on the cars, and perhaps meet people belonging to our church, with a newspaper bundle under her arm.

But her genius for expedients saved her from this humiliation. She had to purchase some sewing-cotton and some other little things, and when she had bought them, she handed her bundle to the woman behind the counter and asked her if she would not be so good as to have that wrapped up with the other things. It was a good deal to ask, she knew, and the woman smiled, for the articles she had bought would not make a package as large as her hand. However, her request was complied with, and she took away a very decent package, with the card of the store stamped on the outside. I suppose that there are not more than half a dozen people in this country who would refuse Euphemia anything that she would be willing to ask for.

So she took the work home, and she labored faith-fully at it for about a week. She did not suppose it would take her so long; but she was not used to such very plain sewing, and was much afraid that she would not do it neatly enough. Besides this, she could only work on it in the daytime,—when I was away,—and was, of course, interrupted a great deal by her ordinary household duties and the necessity of a careful oversight of Pomona's somewhat erratic methods of doing her work.

But at last she finished the job and took it into the city. She did not want to spend any more money on the trip than was absolutely necessary, and so was very glad to find that she had a remnant of pocket-money sufficient to pay her fare both ways.

When she reached the city, she walked up to the

place where her work was to be delivered, and found it much farther when she went on foot than it had seemed to her riding in the street-cars. She handed over her bundle to the proper person, and, as it was soon examined and approved, she received her pay therefor.

It amounted to sixty cents. She had made no bargain, but she was a little astonished. However, she said nothing, but left the place without asking for any more work. In fact, she forgot all about it. She had an idea that everything was all wrong, and that idea engrossed her mind entirely. There was no mistake about the sum paid, for the lady clerk had referred to the printed table of prices when she calculated the amount due. But something was wrong, and at the moment Euphemia could not tell what it was. She left the place, and started to walk back to the ferry. But she was so tired and weak and hungry —it was now an hour or two past her regular luncheon-time—that she thought she should faint if she did not go somewhere and get some refreshments.

So, like a sensible little woman as she was, she went into a restaurant. She sat down at a table, and a waiter came to her to see what she would have. She was not accustomed to eating-houses, and perhaps this was the first time that she had ever visited one alone. What she wanted was something simple. So she ordered a cup of tea and some rolls, and a piece of chicken. The meal was a very good one, and Euphemia enjoyed it. When she had finished she went up to the counter to settle. Her bill was sixty cents. She paid the money she had just received, and walked down to the ferry—all in a daze, she said.

When she got home she thought it over, and then she cried.

After a while she dried her eyes, and when I came home she told me all about it.

"I give it up," she said. "I don't believe I can help you any."

Poor little thing! I took her in my arms and comforted her, and before bedtime I had convinced her that she was fully able to help me better than any one else on earth, and that without puzzling her brains about business, or wearing herself out by sewing for pay.

So we went on in our old way, and by keeping our attention on our weekly balance we prevented it from growing very rapidly.

We fell back on our philosophy,—it was all the capital we had,—and became as calm and contented as circumstances allowed.

CHAPTER V

POMONA PRODUCES A PARTIAL REVOLUTION
IN RUDDER GRANGE

EUPHEMIA began to take a great deal of comfort in her girl. Every evening she had some new instance to relate of Pomona's inventive abilities and aptness in adapting herself to the peculiarities of our method of housekeeping. "Only to think!" said she, one afternoon. "Pomona has just done another *very* smart thing. You know what a trouble it has always been for us to carry all our waste water up-stairs and throw it over the bulwarks. Well, she has remedied all that. She has cut a nice little low window in the side of the kitchen, and has made a shutter of the piece she cut out, with leather hinges to it, and now she can just open this window, throw the water out, shut it again, and there it is! I tell you, she's smart."

"Yes, there is no doubt of that," I said; "but I think that there is danger of her taking more interest in such extraordinary and novel duties than in the regular work of the house."

"Now, don't discourage the girl, my dear," she said, "for she is of the greatest use to me, and I don't want you to be throwing cold water about like some people."

"Not even if I throw it out of Pomona's little door, I suppose."

"No. Don't throw it at all. Encourage people. What would the world be if everybody chilled our aspirations and extraordinary efforts? Like Fulton's steamboat!"

"All right," I said, "I'll not discourage her."

It was now getting late in the season. It was quite too cool to sit out on deck in the evening, and our garden began to look desolate.

Our boarder had wheeled up a lot of fresh earth, and had prepared a large bed, in which he had planted turnips. They made an excellent fall crop, he assured us.

From being simply cool it began to be rainy, and the weather grew decidedly unpleasant. But our boarder bade us take courage. This was probably the "equinoctial," and when it was over there would be a delightful Indian summer, and the turnips would grow nicely.

This sounded very well, but the wind blew up cold at night, and there was a great deal of unpleasant rain.

One night it blew what Pomona called a "whirli-cane," and we went to bed very early to keep warm. We heard our boarder on deck in the garden after we were in bed, and Euphemia said she could not imagine what he was about, unless he was anchoring his turnips to keep them from blowing away.

During the night I had a dream. I thought I was a boy again, and was trying to stand upon my head, a feat for which I had been famous. But instead of throwing myself forward on my hands, and then raising my heels backward over my head, in the orthodox manner, I was on my back, and trying to get on my head from that position. I awoke suddenly, and found that the foot-board of the bedstead was much higher than our heads. We were lying on a very much inclined plane, with our heads downward. I roused Euphemia, and we both got out of bed, when, at almost the same moment, we slipped down the floor into ever so much water.

Euphemia was scarcely awake, and she fell down gurgling. It was dark, but I heard her fall, and I jumped over the bedstead to her assistance. I had scarcely raised her up when I heard a pounding at the front door, or main-hatchway, and our boarder shouted:

"Get up! Come out of that! Open the door! The old boat's turning over!"

My heart fell within me, but I clutched Euphemia. I said no word, and she simply screamed. I dragged her over the floor, sometimes in the water and sometimes out of it. I got the dining-room door open and set her on the stairs. They were in a topsy-turvy condition, but they were dry. I found a lantern which hung on a nail, with a match-box under it, and I struck a light. Then I scrambled back and brought her some clothes.

All this time the boarder was yelling and pounding at the door. When Euphemia was ready I opened the door and took her out.

"You go dress yourself," said the boarder. "I'll hold her here until you come back."

I left her and found my clothes, which, chair and all, had tumbled against the foot of the bed and so had not gone into the water, and soon reappeared on deck. The wind was blowing strongly, but it did not now seem to be very cold. The deck reminded me of the gang-plank of a Harlem steamboat at low tide. It was inclined at an angle of more than forty-five degrees, I am sure. There was light enough for us to see about us, but the scene and all the dreadful circumstances made me feel the most intense desire to wake up and find it all a dream. There was no doubt, however, about the boarder being wide awake.

"Now, then," said he, "take hold of her on that side and we'll help her over here. You scramble down on that side,—it's all dry just there; the boat's turned over toward the water,—and I'll lower her down to you. I'll let a rope over the sides. You can hold on to that as you go down."

I got over the bulwarks and let myself down to the ground. Then the boarder got Euphemia up and slipped her over the side, holding to her hands, and letting her gently down until I could reach her. She said never a word, but screamed at times. I carried her a little way up the shore and set her down. I wanted to take her up to a house near by, where we bought our milk, but she declined to go until we had saved Pomona.

So I went back to the boat, having carefully wrapped up Euphemia, to endeavor to save the girl. I found that the boarder had so arranged the gang-plank that it was possible, without a very great exercise of agility, to pass from the shore to the boat. When I first saw him, on reaching the shelving deck, he was staggering up the stairs with a dining-room chair and a large framed engraving of Raphael's

RUDDER GRANGE

"Dante"—an ugly picture, but full of true feeling, at least, so Euphemia always declared, though I am not quite sure that I know what she meant.

"Where is Pomona?" I said, endeavoring to stand on the hillside of the deck.

"I don't know," said he, "but we must get the things out. The tide's rising and the wind's getting up. The boat will go over before we know it."

"But we must find the girl," I said. "She can't be left to drown."

"I don't think it would matter much," said he, getting over the side of the boat with his awkward load. "She would be of about as much use drowned as any other way. If it hadn't been for that hole she cut in the side of the boat, this would never have happened."

"You don't think it was that!" I said, holding the picture and the chair while he let himself down to the gang-plank.

"Yes, it was," he replied. "The tide's very high, and the water got over that hole and rushed in. The water and the wind will finish this old craft before very long."

Then he took his load from me and dashed down the gang-plank. I went below to look for Pomona. The lantern still hung on the nail, and I took it down and went into the kitchen. There was Pomona, dressed and with her hat on, quietly packing some things in a basket.

"Come, hurry out of this," I cried. "Don't you know that this house—this boat, I mean—is a wreck?"

"Yes, sma'am,—sir, I mean,—I know it, and I suppose we shall soon be at the mercy of the waves."

53

"Well, then, go as quickly as you can. What are you putting in that basket?"

"Food," she said. "We may need it."

I took her by the shoulder and hurried her on deck, over the bulwark, down the gang-plank, and so on to the place where I had left Euphemia.

I found the dear girl there, quiet and collected, all up in a little bunch to shield herself from the wind. I wasted no time, but hurried her and Pomona over to the house of our milk-merchant. There, with some difficulty, I roused the good woman, and after seeing Euphemia and Pomona safely in the house, I left them to tell the tale, and ran back to the boat.

The boarder was working like a Trojan, and had already a pile of our furniture on the beach.

I set about helping him, and for an hour we labored at this hasty and toilsome moving. It was indeed a toilsome business. The floors were shelving, the stairs leaned over sidewise ever so far, and the gang-plank was desperately short and steep.

Still, we saved quite a number of household articles. Some things we broke and some we forgot, and some things were too big to move in this way; but we did very well, considering the circumstances.

The wind roared, the tide rose, and the boat groaned and creaked. We were in the kitchen, trying to take the stove apart, for the boarder was sure we could carry it up, if we could get the pipe out and the legs and doors off, when we heard a crash. We rushed on deck, and found that the garden had fallen in! Making our way as well as we could toward the gaping rent in the deck, we saw that the turnip-bed had gone down bodily into the boarder's room. He did not hesitate, but scrambled down his narrow stairs. I followed him. He struck a match that he had in his pocket, and lighted a little lantern that hung under the stairs. His room was a perfect rubbish-heap. The floor, bed, chairs, pitcher, basin—everything was covered or filled with garden mold and turnips. Never did I behold such a scene. He stood in the midst of it, holding his lantern high above his head. At length he spoke.

"If we had time," he said, "we might come down here and pick out a lot of turnips."

"But how about your furniture?" I exclaimed.

"Oh, that's ruined!" he replied.

So we did not attempt to save any of it, but we got hold of his trunk and carried that on shore.

When we returned, we found that the water was pouring through his partition, making the room a lake of mud. And, as the water was rising rapidly below, and the boat was keeling over more and more, we thought it was time to leave, and we left.

It would not do to go far away from our possessions, which were piled up in a sad-looking heap on the shore; and so, after I had gone over to the milk-woman's to assure Euphemia of our safety, the boarder and I passed the rest of the night—there was not much of it left—in walking up and down the beach smoking some cigars which he fortunately had in his pocket.

In the morning I took Euphemia to the hotel, about a mile away, and arranged for the storage of our furniture there until we could find another habitation. This habitation, we determined, was to be in a substantial house, or part of a house, which should not be affected by the tides.

During the morning the removal of our effects was successfully accomplished, and our boarder went to town to look for a furnished room. He had nothing but his trunk to take to it.

In the afternoon I left Euphemia at the hotel, where she was taking a nap,—she certainly needed it, for she had spent the night in a wooden rocking-chair at the milk-woman's,—and I strolled down to the river to take a last look at the remains of old Rudder Grange.

I felt sad enough as I walked along the well-worn path to the canal-boat, and thought how it had been worn by my feet more than any other's, and how gladly I had walked that way so often during that delightful summer. I forgot all that had been disagreeable, and thought only of the happy times we had had.

It was a beautiful autumn afternoon, and the wind had entirely died away. When I came within sight of our old home, it presented a doleful appearance. The bow had drifted out into the river, and was almost entirely under water. The stern stuck up in a mournful and ridiculous manner, with its keel, instead of its broadside, presented to the view of persons on the shore. As I neared the boat I heard a voice. I stopped and listened. There was no one in sight. Could the sounds come from the boat? I concluded that it must be so, and I walked up closer. Then I heard distinctly the words:

"He grasp ed her by the thro at and yell ed, 'Swear to me thou nev er wilt re veal my se cret, or thy hot heart's blood shall stain this mar bel flo or.' She gave one gry vy ous gasp and—"

It was Pomona!

Doubtless she had climbed up the stern of the boat and had descended into the depths of the wreck to rescue her beloved book, the reading of which had so long been interrupted by my harsh decrees. Could I break in on this one hour of rapture? I had not the heart to do it, and as I slowly moved away, there came to me the last words that I ever heard from Rudder Grange:

"And with one wild shry ik to heav en her heart's blo od spat ter ed that prynce ly home of woe—"

CHAPTER VI

THE NEW RUDDER GRANGE

I HAVE before given an account of the difficulties we encountered when we started out house-hunting, and it was this doleful experience which made Euphemia declare that before we set out on a second search for a residence we should know exactly what we wanted.

To do this, we must know how other people lived, we must examine into the advantages and disadvantages of the various methods of housekeeping, and make up our minds on the subject.

When we came to this conclusion we were in a city boarding-house, and were entirely satisfied that this style of living did not suit us at all.

At this juncture I received a letter from the gentleman who had boarded with us on the canal-boat. Shortly after leaving us the previous fall, he had married a widow lady with two children, and was now keeping house in a French flat in the upper part of the city. We had called upon the happy couple soon after their marriage, and the letter now received contained an invitation for us to come and dine, and spend the night.

"We'll go," said Euphemia. "There's nothing I

want so much as to see how people keep house in a French flat. Perhaps we'll like it. And I must see those children." So we went.

The house, as Euphemia remarked, was anything but flat. It was very tall indeed—the tallest house in the neighborhood. We entered the vestibule, the outer door being open, and beheld, on one side of us, a row of bell-handles. Above each of these handles was the mouth of a speaking-tube, and above each of these a little glazed frame containing a visiting-card.

"Isn't this cute?" said Euphemia, reading over the cards. "Here's his name, and this is his bell and tube! Which would you do first, ring or blow?"

"My dear," said I, "you don't blow up those tubes. We must ring the bell, just as if it were an ordinary front-door bell, and instead of coming to the door, some one will call down the tube to us."

I rang the bell under the boarder's name, and very soon a voice at the tube said:

"Well?"

Then I told our names, and in an instant the front door opened.

"Why, their flat must be right here," whispered Euphemia. "How quickly the girl came!" She looked for the girl as we entered, but there was no one there.

"Their flat is on the fifth story," said I. "He mentioned that in his letter. We would better shut the door and go up."

Up and up the softly carpeted stairs we climbed, and not a soul we saw or heard.

"It is like an enchanted cavern," said Euphemia. "You say the magic word, the door in the rock opens, and you go on and on through the vaulted passages—"

"Until you come to the ogre," said the boarder, who was standing at the top of the stairs. He did not behave at all like an ogre, for he was very glad to see us, and so was his wife. After we had settled down in the parlor, and the boarder's wife had gone to see about something concerning the dinner, Euphemia asked after the children.

"I hope they haven't gone to bed," she said, "for I do so want to see the dear little things."

The ex-boarder, as Euphemia called him, smiled grimly.

"They're not so very little," he said. "My wife's son is nearly grown. He is at an academy in Connecticut, and he expects to go into a civil engineer's office in the spring. His sister is older than he is. My wife married—in the first instance—when she was very young—very young indeed."

"Oh!" said Euphemia; and then, after a pause, "And neither of them is at home now?"

"No," said the ex-boarder. "By the way, what do you think of this dado? It is a portable one; I devised it myself. You can take it away with you to another house when you move. But there is the dinner-bell. I'll show you over the establishment after we have had something to eat."

After our meal we made a tour of inspection. The flat, which included the whole floor, contained nine or ten rooms, of all shapes and sizes. The corners in some of the rooms were cut off and shaped up into closets and recesses, so that Euphemia said the corners of every room were in some other room.

RUDDER GRANGE

Near the back of the flat was a dumb-waiter, with bells and speaking-tubes. When the butcher, the baker, or the kerosene-lamp maker, came each morning, he rang the bell and called up the tube to know what was wanted. The order was called down, and he brought the things in the afternoon.

All this greatly charmed Euphemia. It was so cute, so complete. There were no interviews with disagreeable tradespeople, none of the ordinary annoyances of housekeeping. Everything seemed to be done with a bell, a speaking-tube, or a crank.

"Indeed," said the ex-boarder, "if it were not for people tripping over the wires, I could rig up attachments by which I could sit in the parlor, and by using pedals and a keyboard, I could do all the work of this house without getting out of my easy-chair."

One of the most peculiar features of the establishment was the servant's room. This was at the rear end of the floor, and as there was not much space left after the other rooms had been made, it was very small—so small, indeed, that it would accommodate only a very short bedstead. This made it necessary for our friends to consider the size of the servant when they engaged her.

"There were several excellent girls at the intelligence office where I called," said the ex-boarder, "but I measured them, and they were all too tall. So we had to take a short one who is only so-so. There was one big Scotch girl who was the very person for us, and I would have taken her if my wife had not objected to my plan for her accommodation."

"What was that?" I asked.

61

"Well," said he, "I first thought of cutting a hole in the partition wall at the foot of the bed, for her to put her feet through."

"Never!" said his wife, emphatically. "I would never have allowed that."

"And then," continued he, "I thought of turning the bed around, and cutting a larger hole, through which she might have put her head into the little room on this side. A low table could have stood under the hole, and her head might have rested on a cushion on the table very comfortably."

"My dear," said his wife, "it would have frightened me to death to go into that room and see that head on a cushion on a table—"

"Like John the Baptist," interrupted Euphemia.

"Well," said our ex-boarder, "the plan would have had its advantages."

"Oh!" cried Euphemia, looking out of a back window. "What a lovely little iron balcony! Do you sit out there on warm evenings?"

"That's a fire-escape," said the ex-boarder. "We don't go out there unless it is very hot indeed, on account of the house being on fire. You see, there is a little door in the floor of the balcony, and an iron ladder leading to the balcony beneath, and so on, down to the first story."

"And you have to creep through that hole and go down that dreadful steep ladder every time there is a fire?" said Euphemia.

"Well, I think we would never go down but once," he answered.

"No, indeed," said Euphemia, "you'd fall down and break your neck the first time;" and she turned away from the window with a very grave expression on her face.

Soon after this our hostess conducted Euphemia to the guest-chamber, while her husband and I finished a bedtime cigar.

When I joined Euphemia in her room, she met me with a mysterious expression on her face. She shut the door, and then said in a very earnest tone:

"Do you see that little bedstead in the corner? I did not notice it until I came in just now, and then, being quite astonished, I said, 'Why, here's a child's bed; who sleeps here?' 'Oh,' said she, 'that's our little Adele's bedstead. We have it in our room when she's here.' 'Little Adele!' said I. 'I didn't know she was little—not small enough for that bed, at any rate.' 'Why, yes,' said she, 'Adele is only four years old. The bedstead is quite large enough for her.' 'And she is not here now?' I said, utterly amazed at all this. 'No,' she answered; 'she is not here now; but we try to have her with us as much as we can, and always keep her little bed ready for her.' 'I suppose she's with her father's people,' I said, and she answered, 'Oh, yes,' and bade me good night. What does all this mean? Our boarder told us that the daughter is grown up, and here his wife declares that she is only four years old! I don't know what in the world to make of this mystery!"

I could give Euphemia no clew. I supposed there was some mistake, and that was all I could say, except that I was sleepy, and that we could find out all about it in the morning. But Euphemia could not dismiss the subject from her mind. She said no more, but I could see, until I fell asleep, that she was thinking about it.

It must have been about the middle of the night, perhaps later, when I was suddenly awakened by Euphemia starting up in the bed with the exclamation:

"I have it!"

"What?" I cried, sitting up in a great hurry. "What is it? What have you got? What's the matter?"

"I know it!" she said, "I know it! Our boarder is a *grandfather!* Little Adele is the grown-up daughter's child. He was quite particular to say that his wife married *very* young. Just to think of it! So short a time ago he was living with us, a bachelor; and now, in four short months, he is a grandfather!"

Carefully propounded inquiries, in the morning, proved Euphemia's conclusions to be correct.

The next evening, when we were quietly sitting in our own room, Euphemia remarked that she did not wish to have anything to do with French flats.

"They seem to be very convenient," I said.

"Oh, yes, convenient enough, but I don't like them. I would hate to live where everything let down like a table-lid, or else turned with a crank. And when I think of those fire-escapes and the boarder's grandchild, it makes me feel very unpleasant."

"But the grandchild doesn't follow as a matter of course," said I.

"No," she answered, "but I shall never like French flats."

And we discussed them no more.

For some weeks we examined into every style of

economic and respectable housekeeping, and many methods of living in what Euphemia called "imitation comfort" were set aside as unworthy of consideration.

"My dear," said Euphemia, one evening, "what we really ought to do is to build. Then we would have exactly the house we want."

"Very true," I replied; "but to build a house a man must have money."

"Oh, no!" said she, "or, at least, not much. For one thing, you might join a building association. In some of those societies I know that you only have to pay a dollar a week."

"But do you suppose the association builds houses for all its members?" I asked.

"Of course I suppose so. Else why is it called a building association?"

I had read a good deal about these organizations, and I explained to Euphemia that a dollar a week was never received by any of them in payment for a new house.

"Then build yourself," she said. "I know how that can be done."

"Oh, it's easy enough," I remarked, "if you have the money."

"No, you needn't have any money," said Euphemia, rather hastily. "Just let me show you. Supposing, for instance, that you want to build a house worth, well, say twenty thousand dollars, in some pretty town near the city."

"I would rather figure on a cheaper house than that for a country place," I interrupted.

"Well, then, say two thousand dollars. You get

masons, and carpenters, and people to dig the cellar, and you engage them to build your house. You needn't pay them until it's done, of course. Then, when it's all finished, borrow two thousand dollars and give the house as security. After that, you see, you have only to pay the interest on the borrowed money. When you save enough money to pay back the loan, the house is your own. Now, isn't that a good plan?"

"Yes," said I, "if there could be found people who would build your house and wait for their money until some one would lend you its full value on a mortgage."

"Well," said Euphemia, "I guess they could be found, if you would only look for them."

"I'll look for them when I go to heaven," I said.

We gave up, for the present, the idea of building or buying a house, and determined to rent a small place in the country, and then, as Euphemia wisely said, if we liked it we might buy it. After she had dropped her building projects she thought that one ought to know just how a house would suit before having it on one's hands.

We could afford something better than a canal-boat now, and therefore we were not so restricted as in our first search for a house. But the one thing which troubled my wife, and, indeed, caused me much anxious thought, was that scourge of almost all rural localities—tramps. It would be necessary for me to be away all day, and we could not afford to keep a man; so we must be careful to get a house somewhere off the line of ordinary travel, or else in a well-settled neighborhood, where there would be some one near at hand in case of unruly visitors.

RUDDER GRANGE

"A village I don't like," said Euphemia. "There is always so much gossip, and people know all about what you have and what you do. And yet, it would be very lonely, and perhaps dangerous, for us to live off somewhere, all by ourselves. There is another objection to a village. We don't want a house with a small yard and a garden at the back. We ought to have a dear little farm, with some fields for corn, and a cow, and a barn, and things of that sort. All that would be lovely. I'll tell you what we want," she cried, seized with a sudden inspiration : "we ought to try to get the end house of a village. Then our house could be near the neighbors, and our farm could stretch out a little way into the country beyond us. Let us fix our minds upon such a house, and I believe we can get it."

So we fixed our minds ; but in the course of a week or two we unfixed them several times to allow the consideration of places which otherwise would have been out of range ; and during one of these intervals of mental disfixment we took a house.

It was not the end house of a village, but it was in the outskirts of a very small rural settlement. Our nearest neighbor was within vigorous shouting distance, and the house suited us so well in other respects that we concluded that this would do. The house was small, but large enough. There were some trees around it, and a little lawn in front. There was a garden, a small barn and stable, a pasture-field, and land enough besides for small patches of corn and potatoes. The rent was low, the water good, and no one can imagine how delighted we were.

We did not furnish the whole house at first. but

what mattered it? We had no horse nor cow, but the pasture and barn were ready for them. We did not propose to begin with everything at once.

Our first evening in that house was made up of hours of unalloyed bliss. We walked from room to room; we looked out on the garden and the lawn; we sat on the little porch while I smoked.

"We were happy at Rudder Grange," said Euphemia; "but that was only a canal-boat, and could not, in the nature of things, have been a permanent home."

"No," said I, "it could not have been permanent; but in many respects it was a delightful home. The very name of it brings pleasant thoughts."

"It was a nice name," said Euphemia, "and I'll tell you what we might do: let us call this place 'Rudder Grange'—the 'New Rudder Grange'! The name will do just as well for a house as for a boat."

I agreed on the spot, and the house was christened.

Our household was small: we had a servant—a German woman—and we had ourselves; that was all.

I did not do much in the garden; it was too late in the season. The former occupant had planted some corn and potatoes, with a few other vegetables, and these I weeded and hoed, working early in the morning and when I came home in the afternoon. Euphemia tied up the rose-vines, trimmed the bushes, and with a little rake and hoe she prepared a flower-bed in front of the parlor window. This exercise gave us splendid appetites, and we loved our new home more and more.

Our German girl did not suit us exactly at first, and day by day she grew to suit us less. She was a quiet, kindly, pleasant creature, and delighted in an

out-of-door life. She was as willing to weed in the
garden as she was to cook or wash. At first I was
very much pleased with this, because, as I remarked
to Euphemia, you can find very few girls who would
be willing to work in the garden, and she might be
made very useful.

But after a time Euphemia began to get a little
out of patience with her. She worked out of doors
entirely too much. And what she did there, as well
as some of her work in the house, was very much like
certain German literature—you did not know how it
was done, or what it was for.

One afternoon I found Euphemia quite annoyed.

"Look here," she said, "and see what that girl has
been at work at nearly all this afternoon. I was
up-stairs sewing, and thought she was ironing. Isn't it
too provoking?"

It *was* provoking. The contemplative German had
collected a lot of short ham-bones,—where she found
them I cannot imagine,—and had made of them a
border around my wife's flower-bed. The bones stuck
up straight a few inches above the ground all along
the edge of the bed, and the marrow cavity of each
one was filled with earth in which she had planted
seeds.

"'These,' she says, 'will spring up and look beautiful,'" said Euphemia. "They have that style of thing
in her country."

"Then let her take them off with her to her country!" I exclaimed.

"No, no," said Euphemia, hurriedly, "don't kick
them out. It would only wound her feelings. She
did it all for the best, and thought it would please me

69

to have such a border around my bed. But she is too independent, and neglects her proper work. I will give her a week's notice and get another servant. When she goes we can take these horrid bones away. But I hope nobody will call on us in the meantime."

"Must we keep these things here a whole week?" I asked.

"Oh, I can't turn her away without giving her a fair notice. That would be cruel."

I saw the truth of the remark, and determined to bear with the bones and her rather than be unkind.

That night Euphemia informed the girl of her decision, and the next morning, soon after I had left, the good German appeared with her bonnet on and her carpet-bag in her hand, to take leave of her mistress.

"What!" cried Euphemia. "You are not going to-day?"

"If it is goot to go at all, it is goot to go now," said the girl.

"And you will go off and leave me without any one in the house, after my putting myself out to give you a fair notice? It's shameful!"

"I think it is very goot for me to go now," quietly replied the girl. "This house is very loneful. I will go to-morrow in the city to see your husband for my money. Goot morning." And off she trudged to the station.

Before I reached the house that afternoon, Euphemia rushed out to tell this story. I would not like to say how far I kicked those ham-bones.

This German girl had several successors, and some of them suited as badly and left as abruptly as herself;

but Euphemia never forgot the ungrateful stab given her by this "ham-bone girl," as she always called her. It was her first wound of the kind, and it came in the very beginning of the campaign, when she was all unused to this domestic warfare.

CHAPTER VII

TREATING OF AN UNSUCCESSFUL BROKER
AND A DOG

It was a couple of weeks, or thereabouts, after this episode that Euphemia came down to the gate to meet me on my return from the city. I noticed a very peculiar expression on her face. She looked both thoughtful and pleased. Almost the first words she said to me were these:

"A tramp came here to-day."

"I am sorry to hear that," I exclaimed. "That's the worst news I have had yet. I did hope that we were far enough from the line of travel to escape these scourges. How did you get rid of him? Was he impertinent?"

"You must not feel that way about all tramps," said she. "Sometimes they are deserving of our charity, and ought to be helped. There is a great difference in them."

"That may be," I said; "but what of this one? When was he here, and when did he go?"

"He did not go at all. He is here now."

"Here now!" I cried. "Where is he?"

"Do not call out so loudly," said Euphemia, putting

her hand on my arm. "You will waken him. He is asleep."

"Asleep!" said I. "A tramp? Here?"

"Yes. Stop; let me tell you about him. He told me his story, and it is a sad one. He is a middle-aged man,—fifty, perhaps,—and has been rich. He was once a broker in Wall Street, but lost money by the failure of various railroads—the Camden and Amboy, for one."

"That hasn't failed," I interrupted.

"Well, then it was the Northern Pacific, or some other one of them,—at any rate, I know it was either a railroad or a bank,—and he soon became very poor. He has a son in Cincinnati, who is a successful merchant, and lives in a fine house, with horses and carriages, and all that, and this poor man has written to his son, but has never had any answer. So now he is going to walk to Cincinnati to see him. He knows he will not be turned away if he can once meet his son face to face. He was very tired when he stopped here,—and he has ever and ever so far to walk yet, you know,—and so after I had given him something to eat I let him lie down in the outer kitchen, on that roll of rag-carpet that is there. I spread it out for him. It is a hard bed for one who has known comfort, but he seems to sleep soundly."

"Let me see him," said I, and I walked back to the outer kitchen.

There lay the unsuccessful broker, fast asleep. His face, which was turned toward me as I entered, showed that it had been many days since he had been shaved, and his hair had apparently been uncombed for about the same length of time. His clothes were very old, and a good deal torn, and he wore one boot and one shoe.

"Whew!" said I. "Have you been giving him whiskey?"

"No," whispered Euphemia, "of course not. I noticed that smell, and he said he had been cleaning his clothes with alcohol."

"They needed it, I'm sure," I remarked as I turned away. "And now," said I, "where's the girl?"

"This is her afternoon out. What is the matter? You look frightened."

"Oh, I'm not frightened, but I find I must go down to the station again. Just run up and put on your bonnet. It will be a nice little walk for you."

I had been rapidly revolving the matter in my mind. What was I to do with this wretch who was now asleep in my outer kitchen? If I woke him up and drove him off,—and I might have difficulty in doing it,—there was every reason to believe that he would not go far, but return at night and commit some revengeful act. I never saw a more sinister-looking fellow. And he was certainly drunk. He must not be allowed to wander about our neighborhood. I would go for the constable and have him arrested.

So I locked the door from the kitchen into the house, and then the outside door of the kitchen, and when my wife came down we hurried off. On the way I told her what I intended to do, and what I thought of our guest. She answered scarcely a word, and I hoped that she was frightened. I think she was.

The constable, who was also coroner of our township, had gone to a creek three miles away to hold an inquest, and there was nobody to arrest the man. The nearest police station was at Hackingford, six miles away, on the railroad. I held a consultation with the station master and the gentleman who kept the grocery store opposite.

They could think of nothing to be done except to shoot the man, and to that I objected.

"However," said 1, "he can't stay there;" and a happy thought just then strik ng me, I called to the boy who drove the village express-wagon, and engaged him for a job. The wagon was standing at the station, and to save time I got in and rode to my house. Euphemia went over to call on the groceryman's wife until I returned.

I had determined that the man should be taken away, although, until I was riding home, I had not made up my mind where to have him taken. But on the road I settled this matter.

On reaching the house, we drove into the yard as close to the kitchen as we could go. Then I unlocked the door, and the boy—who was a big, strapping fellow —entered with me. We found the ex-broker still wrapped in the soundest slumber. Leaving the boy to watch him, I went up-stairs and got a baggage tag, which I directed to the chief of police at the police station in Hackingford. I returned to the kitchen, and fastened this tag conspicuously on the lapel of the sleeper's coat. Then, with a clothes-line, I tied him up carefully, hand and foot. To all this he offered not the slightest opposition. When he was suitably packed, with due regard to the probable tenderness of wrist and ankle in one brought up in luxury, the boy and I carried him to the wagon.

75

He was a heavy load, and we may have bumped him a little, but his sleep was not disturbed. Then we drove him to the express office. This was at the railroad-station, and the station master was also express agent. At first he was not inclined to receive my parcel; but when I assured him that all sorts of live things were sent by express, and that I could see no reason for making an exception in this case, he added my arguments to his own disposition as a householder to see the goods forwarded to their destination, and so gave me a receipt, and pasted a label on the ex-broker's shoulder. I set no value on the package, which I prepaid.

"Now, then," said the station master, "he'll go all right, if the express agent on the train will take him."

This matter was soon settled, for in a few minutes the train stopped at the station. My package was wheeled to the express-car, and two porters, who entered heartily into the spirit of the thing, hoisted it into the car. The train agent, who just then noticed the character of the goods, began to declare that he would not have the fellow in his car; but my friend the station master shouted out that everything was all right,—the man was properly packed, invoiced, and paid for,—and the train, which was behind time, moved away before the irate agent could take measures to get rid of his unwelcome freight.

"Now," said I, "there'll be a drunken man at the police station in Hackingford in about half an hour. His offense will be as evident there as here, and they can do what they please with him. I shall telegraph to explain the matter and prepare them for his arrival."

76

RUDDER GRANGE

When I had done this Euphemia and I went home. The tramp had cost me some money, but I was well satisfied with my evening's work, and felt that the township owed me at least a vote of thanks.

But I firmly made up my mind that Euphemia should never again be left unprotected. I would not even trust to a servant who would agree to have no afternoons out. I would get a dog.

The next day I advertised for a fierce watch-dog, and in the course of a week I got one. Before I procured him I examined into the merits and price of about one hundred dogs. My dog was named Pete, but I determined to make a change in that respect. He was a very tall, bony, powerful beast, of a dull black color, and with a lower jaw that would crack the hind leg of an ox, so I was informed. He was of a varied breed, and the good Irishman of whom I bought him said he had fine blood in him, and attempted to refer him back to the different classes of dogs from which he had been derived. But after I had had him awhile, I made an analysis based on his appearance and character, and concluded that he was mainly bloodhound, shaded with wolf-dog and mastiff, and picked out with touches of bulldog.

The man brought him home for me, and chained him up in an unused woodshed, for I had no dog-house as yet.

"Now, thin," said he, "all you've got to do is to keep 'im chained up there for three or four days till he gets used to ye. An' I'll tell ye the best way to make a dog like ye. Jist give him a good lickin'. Then he'll know yer his master, an' he'll like ye iver aftherward. There's plenty of people that don't know

77

that. And, by the way, sir, that chain's none too strong for 'im. I got it when he wasn't mor'n half grown. Ye'd betther git him a new one."

When the man had gone, I stood and looked at the dog, and could not help hoping that he would learn to like me without the intervention of a thrashing. Such harsh methods were not always necessary, I felt sure.

After our evening meal—a combination of dinner and supper, of which Euphemia used to say that she did not know whether to call it dinper or supner—we went out together to look at our new guardian.

Euphemia was charmed with him.

"How massive!" she exclaimed. "What splendid limbs! And look at that immense head! I know I shall never be afraid now. I feel he is a dog I can rely upon. Make him stand up, please, so I can see how tall he is."

"I think it would be better not to disturb him," I answered; "he may be tired. He will get up of his own accord very soon. And, indeed, I hope that he will not get up until I go to the store and get him a new chain."

As I said this I made a step forward to look at his chain, and at that instant a low growl, like the first rumblings of an earthquake, ran through the dog.

I stepped back again, and walked over to the village for the chain. The dog-chains shown me at the store all seemed too short and too weak, and I concluded to buy two chains, such as are used for hitching horses, and to join them so as to make a long as well as a strong one of them. I wanted him to be able to come out of the woodshed when it should be necessary to show himself.

On my way home with my purchase the thought

RUDDER GRANGE

suddenly struck me, How will you put that chain on your dog? The memory of the rumbling growl was still vivid.

I never put the chain on him. As I approached him with it in my hand, he rose to his feet, his eyes sparkled, his black lips drew back from his mighty teeth, he gave one savage bark, and sprang at me.

His chain held, and I went into the house. That night he broke loose and went home to his master, who lived fully ten miles away.

When I found in the morning that he was gone, I was in doubt whether it would be better to go and look for him or not. But I concluded to keep up a brave heart, and found him, as I expected, at the place where I had bought him. The Irishman took him to my house again, and I had to pay for the man's loss of time as well as for his fare on the railroad. But the dog's old master chained him up with the new chain, and I felt repaid for my outlay.

Every morning and night I fed that dog, and I spoke as kindly and gently to him as I knew how. But he seemed to cherish a distaste for me, and always greeted me with a growl. He was an awful dog.

About a week after the arrival of this animal, I was astonished and frightened, on nearing the house, to hear a scream from my wife. I rushed into the yard, and was greeted with a succession of screams from two voices, that seemed to come from the vicinity of the woodshed. Hurrying thither, I perceived Euphemia standing on the roof of the shed in perilous proximity to the edge, while near the ridge of the roof sat our hired girl with her handkerchief over her head.

79

"Hurry, hurry!" cried Euphemia. "Climb up here! The dog is loose! Be quick! Be quick! Oh! he's coming, he's coming!"

I asked for no explanation. There was a rail fence by the side of the shed, and I sprang on this, and was on the roof just as the dog came bounding and barking from the barn.

Instantly Euphemia had me in her arms, and we came very near going off the roof together.

"I never feared to have you come home before," she sobbed. "I thought he would tear you limb from limb."

"But how did all this happen?" said I.

"Och! I kin hardly remember," said the girl from under her handkerchief.

"Well, I didn't ask you," I said, somewhat too sharply.

"Oh, I'll tell you," said Euphemia. "There was a man at the gate, and he looked suspicious and didn't try to come in, and Mary was at the barn looking for an egg, and I thought this was a good time to see whether the dog was a good watch-dog or not, so I went and unchained him—"

"Did you unchain that dog?" I cried.

"Yes, and the minute he was loose he made a rush at the gate; but the man was gone before he got there, and as he ran down the road I saw that he was Mr. Henderson's man, who was coming here on an errand, I expect; and then I went down to the barn to get Mary to come and help me chain up the dog, and when she came out he began to chase me and then her; and we were so frightened that we climbed up here, and I don't know, I'm sure, how I ever got up that fence; and do you think he can climb up here?"

"Oh, no, my dear," I said.

"An' he's just the beast to go afther a stip-ladder," said the girl, in muffled tones.

"And what are we to do?" asked Euphemia. "We can't eat and sleep up here. Don't you think that if we were all to shout out together we could make some neighbor hear?"

"Oh, yes!" I said, "there is no doubt of it. But then, if a neighbor came, the dog would fall on him—"

"And tear him limb from limb," interrupted Euphemia.

"Yes, and besides, my dear, I should hate to have any of the neighbors come and find us all up here. It would look so utterly absurd. Let me try to think of some other plan."

"Well, please be as quick as you can. It's dreadful to be—who's that?"

I looked up and saw a female figure just entering the yard.

"Oh, what shall we do?" exclaimed Euphemia. "The dog will get her. Call to her!"

"No, no," said I, "don't make a noise. It will only bring the dog. He seems to have gone to the barn or somewhere. Keep perfectly quiet, and she may go up on the porch; and as the front door is not locked, she may rush into the house if she sees him coming."

"I do hope she will do that," said Euphemia, anxiously.

"And yet," said I, "it's not pleasant to have strangers going into the house when there's no one there."

"But it's better than seeing a stranger torn to pieces before your eyes," said Euphemia.

"Yes," I replied, "it is. Don't you think we might get down now? The dog isn't here."

"No, no!" cried Euphemia. "There he is now, coming this way. And look at that woman! She is coming right to this shed."

Sure enough, our visitor had passed by the front door, and was walking toward us. Evidently she had heard our voices.

"Don't come here!" cried Euphemia. "You'll be killed! Run! run! The dog is coming! Why, mercy on us! It's Pomona!"

CHAPTER VIII

Sure enough, it was Pomona. There stood our old servant-girl of the canal-boat, with a crooked straw bonnet on her head, a faded yellow parasol in her hand, a parcel done up in newspaper under her arm, and an expression of astonishment on her face.

"Well, truly!" she ejaculated.

"Into the house, quick!" I said. "We have a savage dog!"

"And here he is!" cried Euphemia. "Oh, she will be torn to atoms!"

Straight at Pomona came the great black beast, barking furiously. But the girl did not move; she did not even turn her head to look at the dog, who stopped before he reached her, and began to rush wildly around her, barking terribly.

We held our breath. I tried to say "Get out!" or "Lie down!" but my tongue could not form the words.

"Can't you get up here?" gasped Euphemia.

"I don't want to," said the girl.

The dog now stopped barking, and stood looking at Pomona, occasionally glancing up at us. Pomona took not the slightest notice of him.

"Do you know, ma'am," said she to Euphemia,

83

RUDDER GRANGE

"that if I had come here yesterday that dog would have had my life's blood."

"And why don't he have it to-day?" said Euphemia, who, with myself, was utterly amazed at the behavior of the dog.

"Because I know more to-day than I did yesterday," answered Pomona. "It is only this afternoon that I read something, as I was coming here on the cars. This is it," she continued, unwrapping her paper parcel and taking from it one of the two books it contained. "I finished this part just as the cars stopped, and I put my scissors in the place; I'll read it to you."

Standing there with one book still under her arm, the newspaper, half unwrapped from it, hanging down and flapping in the breeze, she opened the other volume at the scissors place, turned back a page or two, and began to read as follows:

"Lord Edward slowly san-ter-ed up the bro-ad anc-es-tral walk, when sudden-ly from out a cop-se, there sprang a fur-i-ous hound. The marsh-man, con-ce-al-ed in a tree expected to see the life's blood of the young nob-le-man stain the path. But no, Lord Edward did not stop nor turn his head. With a smile, he strode stead-i-ly on. Well he knew that if by be-traying no em-otion, he could show the dog that he was walking where he had a right, the bru-te would re-cog-nize that right and let him pass un-sca-thed. Thus in this moment of peril his nob-le courage saved him. The hound, abashed, returned to his cov-ert, and Lord Edward pass-ed on.

" 'Foi-led again,' mutter-ed the marsh-man.''

"Now, then," said Pomona, closing the book, "you see, I remembered that the minute I saw the dog coming, and I didn't betray any emotion. Yesterday,

84

" 'Foiled again,' muttered the marsh-man."

now, when I didn't know it, I'd 'a' been sure to betray emotion, and he would have had my life's blood. Did he drive you up there?"

"Yes," said Euphemia; and she hastily explained the situation.

"Then I guess I'd better chain him up," remarked Pomona; and, advancing to the dog, she took him boldly by the collar and pulled him toward the shed. The animal hung back at first, but soon followed her, and she chained him up securely.

"Now you can come down," said Pomona.

I assisted Euphemia to the ground, and Pomona persuaded the hired girl to descend.

"Will he grab me by the leg?" asked the girl.

"No; get down, gump," said Pomona; and down she scrambled.

We took Pomona into the house with us, and asked her news of herself.

"Well," said she, "there ain't much to tell. I stayed awhile at the institution; but I didn't get much good there—only I learned to read to myself, because if I read out loud they came and took the book away. Then I left there and went to live out. But the woman was awful mean. She throwed away one of my books and I was only half through it. It was a real good book, named 'The Bridal Corpse, or Montregor's Curse,' and I had to pay for it at the circulatin' library. So I left her quick enough, and then I went on the stage."

"On the stage!" cried Euphemia. "What did you do on the stage?"

"Scrub," replied Pomona. "You see I thought if I could get anything to do at the theayter, I could work my way up, so I was glad to get scrubbin'. I asked the prompter, one mornin', if he thought there was a chance for me to work up, and he said yes, I might scrub the galleries; and then I told him that I didn't want none of his lip, and I pretty soon left that place. I heard you was a-keepin' house out here, and so I thought I'd come along and see you, and, if you hadn't no girl, I'd like to live with you again; and I guess you might as well take me, for that other girl said, when she got down from the shed, that she was goin' away to-morrow—she wouldn't stay in no house where they kept such a dog; though I told her I guessed he was only cuttin' round because he was so glad to get loose."

"Cutting around!" exclaimed Euphemia. "It was nothing of the kind. If you had seen him you would have known better. But did you come now to stay? Where are your things?"

"On me," replied Pomona.

When Euphemia found that the Irish girl really intended to leave, we consulted together, and concluded to engage Pomona. I went so far as to agree to carry her books to and from the circulating library to which she subscribed, hoping thereby to be able to exercise some influence on her taste. Thus part of the old family of Rudder Grange had come together again. True, the boarder was away, but as Pomona remarked when she heard about him, "You couldn't always expect to ever regain the ties that had always bound everybody."

Our delight and interest in our little farm increased day by day. In a week or two after Pomona's arrival I bought a cow. Euphemia was very anxious to have

an Alderney,—they were such gentle, beautiful creatures,—but I could not afford such a luxury. I might
possibly compass an Alderney calf, but we would have
to wait a couple of years for our milk, and Euphemia
said it would be better to have a common cow than to
do that.

Great was our inward satisfaction when the cow, our
own cow, walked slowly and solemnly into our yard
and began to crop the clover on our little lawn. Pomona and I gently drove her to the barn, while Euphemia endeavored to quiet the violent demonstrations
of the dog (fortunately chained) by assuring him that
this was *our* cow, and that she was to live here, and
that he was to take care of her and never bark at her.
All this and much more, delivered in the earnest and
confidential tone in which ladies talk to infants and
dumb animals, made the dog think that he was to be
let loose to kill the cow, and he bounded and leaped
with delight, tugging at his chain so violently that
Euphemia became a little frightened and left him.
This dog had been named Lord Edward, at the earnest
solicitation of Pomona, and he was becoming somewhat
reconciled to his life with us. He allowed me to unchain him at night, and I could generally chain him
up in the morning without trouble if I had a good big
plate of food with which to tempt him into the shed.

Before supper we all went down to the barn to see
the milking. Pomona, who knew all about such things,
having been on a farm in her first youth, was to be the
milkmaid. But when she began operations, she did
no more than begin. Milk as industriously as she
might, she got no milk.

"This is a queer cow," said Pomona.

"Are you sure that you know how to milk?" asked Euphemia, anxiously.

"Can I milk?" said Pomona. "Why, of course, ma'am. I've seen 'em milk hundreds of times."

"But you never milked, yourself?" I remarked.

"No, sir, but I know just how it's done."

That might be, but she couldn't do it, and at last we had to give up the matter in despair, and leave the poor cow until morning, when Pomona was to go for a man who occasionally worked on the place, and engage him to come and milk for us.

That night as we were going to bed I looked out of the window at the barn which contained the cow, and was astonished to see that there was a light inside of the building.

"What!" I exclaimed. "Can't we be left in peaceful possession of a cow for a single night?" And taking my revolver, I hurried down-stairs and out of doors, forgetting my hat in my haste. Euphemia screamed after me to be careful to keep the pistol pointed away from me.

I whistled for the dog as I went out, but, to my surprise, he did not answer.

"Has he been killed?" I thought, and, for a moment, I wished I were a large family of brothers—all armed.

But on my way to the barn I met a person approaching with a lantern and a dog. It was Pomona, and she had a milk-pail on her arm.

"See here, sir," she said, "it's mor'n half full. I just made up my mind that I'd learn to milk, if it took me all night. I didn't go to bed at all, and I've been at the barn fur an hour. And there ain't no need of my goin' after no man in the mornin'," said she, hanging up the barn key on its nail.

I simply mention this circumstance to show what kind of a girl Pomona had grown to be.

We were all the time at work, in some way, improving our little place. "Some day we will buy it," said Euphemia. We intended to have some wheat put in in the fall, and next year we would make the place fairly crack with luxuriance. We would divide the duties of the farm, and, among other things, Euphemia would take charge of the chickens. She wished to do this entirely herself, so there might be one thing that should be all her own, just as my work in town was all my own. As she wished to buy the chickens and defray all the necessary expenses out of her own private funds, I could make no objections, and, indeed, I had no desire to do so. She bought a chicken-book, and made herself mistress of the subject. For a week there was a strong chicken flavor in all our conversation.

This was while the poultry-yard was building. There was a chicken-house on the place, but no yard, and Euphemia intended to have a good big one, because she was going into the business to make money.

"Perhaps my chickens may buy the place," she said, and I very much hoped they would.

Everything was to be done very systematically. She would have Leghorns, Brahmas, and common fowls. The first because they laid so many eggs, the second because they were such fine, big fowls, and the third because they were such good mothers.

"We will eat and sell the eggs of the first and third

classes," she said, "and set the eggs of the second class under the hens of the third class."

"There seems to be some injustice in that arrangement," I said, "for the first class will always be childless, the second class will have nothing to do with their offspring, while the third will be obliged to bring up and care for the children of others."

But I really had no voice in this matter. As soon as the carpenter had finished the yard, and had made some coops and other necessary arrangements, Euphemia hired a carriage and went about the country to buy chickens. It was not easy to find just what she wanted, and she was gone all day.

However, she brought home an enormous Brahma cock and ten hens, which number was pretty equally divided into her three classes. She was very proud of her purchases, and indeed they were fine fowls. In the evening I made some allusion to the cost of all this carpenter work, carriage hire, etc., besides the price of the chickens.

"Oh!" said she, "you don't look at the matter in the right light. You haven't studied it up as I have. Now, just let me show you how this thing will pay, if carried on properly." Producing a piece of paper covered with figures, she continued : "I begin with ten hens—I got four common ones, because it would make it easier to calculate. After a while I set these ten hens on thirteen eggs each. Three of these eggs will probably spoil—that leaves ten chickens hatched out. Of these, I will say that half die ; that will make five chickens for each hen. You see, I leave a large margin for loss. This makes fifty chickens, and when we add the ten hens we have sixty fowls at the end of the first year. Next year I set these sixty, and they bring up five chickens each,—I am sure there will be a larger proportion than this, but I want to be safe,— and that is three hundred chickens; add the hens, and we have three hundred and sixty at the end of the second year. In the third year, calculating in the same safe way, we shall have twenty-one hundred and sixty chickens; in the fourth year there will be twelve thousand nine hundred and sixty; and at the end of the fifth year, which is as far as I need to calculate now, we shall have sixty-four thousand and eight hundred fowls. What do you think of that? At seventy-five cents apiece,—which is cheap enough,—that would be forty-eight thousand and six hundred dollars. Now, what is the petty cost of a fence and a few coops by the side of a sum like that?"

"Nothing at all," I answered. "It is lost like a drop in the ocean. I hate, my dear, to interfere in any way with such a splendid calculation as that, but I would like to ask you one question."

"Oh, of course," she said. "I suppose you are going to say something about the cost of feeding all this poultry. That is to come out of the chickens supposed to die. They won't die. It is ridiculous to suppose that each hen will bring up but five chickens. The chickens that will live out of those I consider as dead will more than pay for the feed."

"That is not what I was going to ask you, although of course it ought to be considered. But you know you are only going to set common hens, and you do not intend to raise any. Now, are those four hens to do all the setting and mother-work for five years, and eventually bring up over sixty-four thousand chickens?"

"Well, I did make a mistake there," she said, coloring a little. "I'll tell you what I'll do : I'll set every one of my hens every year."

"But all those chickens may not be hens. You have calculated that every one of them would set as soon as it was old enough."

She stopped a minute to think this over.

"Two heads are better than one, I see," she said directly. "I'll allow that one half of all the chickens are roosters, and that will make the profits twenty-four thousand three hundred dollars—more than enough to buy this place."

"Ever so much more," I cried. "This Rudder Grange is ours!"

CHAPTER IX

My wife and I were both so fond of country life and country pursuits that month after month passed by at our little farm in a succession of delightful days. Time flew like a limited express train, and it was September before we knew it.

I had been working very hard at the office that summer, and was glad to think of my two weeks' vacation, which was to begin on the first Monday of the month. I had intended spending these two weeks in rural retirement at home, but an interview in the city with my family physician caused me to change my mind. I told him my plan.

"Now," said he, "if I were you I would do nothing of the kind. You have been working too hard; your face shows it. You need rest and change. Nothing will do you so much good as to camp out; that will be fifty times better than going to any summer resort. You can take your wife with you. I know she'll like it. I don't care where you go, so that it's a healthy spot. Get a good tent and an outfit, be off to the woods, and forget all about business and domestic matters for a few weeks."

This sounded splendid, and I propounded the plan

93

to Euphemia that evening. She thought very well of it, and was sure we could do it. Pomona would not be afraid to remain in the house, under the protection of Lord Edward, and she could easily attend to the cow and the chickens. It would be a holiday for her, too. Old John, the man who occasionally worked for us, would come up sometimes and see after things. With her customary dexterity, Euphemia swept away every obstacle to the plan, and all was settled before we went to bed.

As my wife had presumed, Pomona made no objections to remaining in charge of the house. The scheme pleased her greatly. So far, so good. I called that day on a friend who was in the habit of camping out, to talk to him about getting a tent and the necessary "traps" for a life in the woods. He proved perfectly competent to furnish advice and everything else. He offered to lend me all I needed. He had a complete outfit; had done with them for the year, and I was perfectly welcome. Here was rare luck. He gave me a tent, camp-stove, dishes, pots, gun, fishing-tackle, a big canvas coat with dozens of pockets riveted on it, a canvas hat, rods, reels, boots that came up to my hips,—about a wagon-load of things in all. He was a really good fellow.

We laid in a stock of canned and condensed provisions, and I bought a book on camping out so as to be well posted on the subject. On the Saturday before the first Monday in September we would have been entirely ready to start had we decided on the place where we were to go.

We found it very difficult to make this decision. There were thousands of places where people went to camp out, but none of them seemed to be the place for us. Most of them were too far away. We figured up the cost of taking ourselves and our camp equipage to the Adirondacks, the Lakes, the trout-streams of Maine, or any of those well-known resorts, and we found that we could not afford such trips, especially for a vacation of but fourteen days.

On Sunday afternoon we took a little walk. Our minds were still troubled about the spot toward which we ought to journey next day, and we needed the soothing influences of nature. The country to the north and west of our little farm was very beautiful. About half a mile from the house a modest river ran ; on each side of it were grass-covered fields and hills, and in some places there were extensive tracts of woodlands.

"Look here !" exclaimed Euphemia, stopping short in the little path that wound along by the river-bank. "Do you see this river, those woods, those beautiful fields, with not a soul in them or anywhere near them, and those lovely blue mountains over there ?" As she spoke she waved her parasol in the direction of the objects indicated, and I could not mistake them. "Now, what could we want better than this ?" she continued. "Here we can fish, and do everything that we want to. I say, let us camp here on our own river. I can take you to the very spot for the tent. Come on !" And she was so excited about it that she fairly ran.

The spot she pointed out was one we had frequently visited in our rural walks. It was a grassy peninsula, as I termed it, formed by a sudden turn of a creek which, a short distance below, flowed into the river.

It was a very secluded spot. The place was approached through a pasture-field,—we had found it by mere accident,—and where the peninsula joined the field,—we had to climb a fence just there,—was a cluster of chestnut and hickory trees, while down near the point stood a wide-spreading oak.

"Here, under this oak, is the place for the tent," said Euphemia, her face flushed, her eyes sparkling, and her dress a little torn by getting over the fence in a hurry. "What do we want with your Adirondacks and your Dismal Swamps? This is the spot for us!"

"Euphemia," said I, in as composed a tone as possible, although my whole frame was trembling with emotion, "Euphemia, I am glad I married you!"

Had it not been Sunday, we would have set up our tent that night.

Early the next morning, Old John's fifteen-dollar horse drew from our house a wagon-load of camp fixtures. There was some difficulty in getting the wagon over the field, and there were fences to be taken down to allow of its passage; but we overcame all obstacles, and reached the camp-ground without breaking so much as a tea-cup. Old John helped me pitch the tent, and as neither of us understood the matter very well, it took us some time. It was, indeed, nearly noon when Old John left us, and it may have been possible that he delayed matters a little so as to be able to charge for a full half-day for himself and horse. Euphemia got into the wagon to ride back with him, that she might give some parting injunctions to Pomona.

"I'll have to stop a bit to put up the fences, ma'am," said Old John, "or Misther Ball might make a fuss."

"Is this Mr. Ball's land?" I asked.

"Oh, yes, sir, it's Mr. Ball's land."

"I wonder how he'll like our camping on it?" I said thoughtfully.

"I'd 'a' thought, sir, you'd 'a' asked him that before you came," said Old John, in a tone that seemed to indicate that he had his doubts about Mr. Ball.

"Oh, there'll be no trouble about that," cried Euphemia. "You can drive me past Mr. Ball's,—it's not much out of the way,—and I'll ask him."

"In that wagon?" said I. "Will you stop at Mr. Ball's door in that?"

"Certainly," said she, as she arranged herself on the board which served as a seat. "Now that our campaign has really commenced, we ought to begin to rough it, and should not be too proud to ride even in a—in a—"

She evidently couldn't think of any vehicle mean enough for her purpose.

"In a green-grocery cart," I suggested.

"Yes, or in a red one. Go ahead, John."

When Euphemia returned on foot, I had a fire in the camp-stove and the kettle was on.

"Well," said Euphemia, "Mr. Ball says it's all right, if we keep the fence up. He don't want his cows to get into the creek, and I'm sure we don't want them walking over us. He couldn't understand, though, why we wanted to live out here. I explained the whole thing to him very carefully, but it didn't seem to make much impression on him. I believe he thinks Pomona has something the matter with her, and that we have come to stay out here in the fresh air so as not to take it."

"What an extremely stupid man Mr. Ball must be!" I exclaimed.

The fire did not burn very well, and while I was at work at it Euphemia spread a cloth upon the grass, and set forth bread and butter, cheese, sardines, potted ham, preserves, biscuits, and a lot of other things.

We did not wait for the kettle to boil, but concluded to do without tea or coffee for this meal, and content ourselves with pure water. For some reason or other, however, the creek water did not seem to be very pure, and we did not like it a bit.

"After lunch," said I, "we will go and look for a spring; that will be a good way of exploring the country."

"If we can't find one," said Euphemia, "we shall have to go to the house for water, for I can never drink that stuff."

Soon after lunch we started out. We searched high and low, near and far, for a spring, but could not find one.

At length, by merest accident, we found ourselves in the vicinity of Old John's little house. I knew he had a good well, and so we went in to get a drink, for our ham and biscuits had made us very thirsty.

We told Old John, who was digging potatoes, and was also very much surprised to see us so soon, about our unexpected trouble in finding a spring.

"No," said he, very slowly, "there is no spring very near to you. Didn't you tell your gal to bring you water?"

"No," I replied, "we don't want her coming down to the camp. She is to attend to the house."

RUDDER GRANGE

"Oh, very well," said John, "I will bring you water, morning and night,—good, fresh water,—from my well, for—well, for ten cents a day."

"That will be nice," said Euphemia, "and cheap, too. And then, it will be well to have John come every day; he can carry our letters."

"I don't expect to write any letters."

"Neither do I," said Euphemia; "but it will be pleasant to have some communication with the outer world."

So we engaged Old John to bring us water twice a day. I was a little disappointed at this, for I thought that camping on the edge of a stream settled the matter of water. But we have many things to learn in this world.

Early in the afternoon I went out to catch some fish for supper. We agreed to dispense with dinner, and have breakfast, lunch, and a good solid supper.

For some time I had poor luck. There were either very few fish in the creek, or they were not hungry.

I had been fishing an hour or more when I saw Euphemia running toward me.

"What's the matter?" said I.

"Oh, nothing. I've just come to see how you were getting along. Haven't you been gone an awfully long time? And are those all the fish you've caught? What little bits of things they are! I thought people who camped out caught big fish and lots of them!"

"That depends a good deal upon where they go," said I.

"Yes, I suppose so," replied Euphemia. "But I should think a stream as big as this would have plenty of fish in it. However, if you can't catch any, you might go up to the road and watch for Mr. Mulligan. He sometimes comes along on Mondays."

"I'm not going to the road to watch for any fish-man," I replied, a little more testily than I should have spoken. "What sort of a camping out would that be? But we must not be talking here, or I shall never get a bite. Those fish are a little soiled from jumping about in the dust. You might wash them off at that shallow place, while I go a little farther on and try my luck."

I went a short distance up the creek, and threw my line into a dark, shadowy pool, under some alders, where there certainly should be fish. And, sure enough, in less than a minute I got a splendid bite —not only a bite, but a pull. I knew I had certainly hooked a big fish! The thing actually tugged at my line so that I was afraid the pole would break. I did not fear for the line, for that, I knew, was strong. I would have played the fish until he was tired and I could pull him out without risk to the pole, but I did not know exactly how the process of "playing" was conducted. I was very much excited. Sometimes I gave a jerk and a pull, and then the fish would give a jerk and a pull.

Directly I heard some one running toward me, and then I heard Euphemia cry out:

"Give him the butt! Give him the butt!"

"Give him what?" I exclaimed, without having time even to look up at her.

"The butt! the butt!" she cried, almost breathlessly. "I know that's right! I read how Edward Everett Hale did it in the Adirondacks."

"Give him the butt! Give him the butt!"

"No, it wasn't Hale at all," said I, as I jumped about the bank; "it was Mr. Murray."

"Well, it was one of those fishing ministers, and I know that it caught the fish."

"I know, I know. I read it, but I don't know how to do it."

"Perhaps you ought to punch him with it," said she.

"No, no!" I hurriedly replied, "I can't do anything like that. I'm going to try to just pull him out lengthwise. You take hold of the pole and go inshore as far as you can, and I'll try and get hold of the line."

Euphemia did as I bade her, and drew the line in so that I could reach it. As soon as I had a firm hold of it, I pulled in, regardless of consequences, and hauled ashore an enormous catfish.

"Hurrah!" I shouted, "here is a prize."

Euphemia dropped the pole, and ran to me.

"What a horrid beast!" she exclaimed. "Throw it in again."

"Not at all!" said I. "This is a splendid fish, if I can ever get him off the hook. Don't come near him! If he sticks that back-fin into you, it will poison you."

"Then I should think it would poison us to eat him," said she.

"No; it's only his fin."

"I've eaten catfish, but I never saw one like that," she said. "Look at its horrible mouth! And it has whiskers like a cat!"

"Oh! you never saw one with its head on," I said. "What I want to do is to get this hook out."

I had caught catfish before, but never one so large as this, and I was actually afraid to take hold of it,

knowing as I did that you must be very careful how
you clutch a fish of the kind. I finally concluded to
carry it home as it was, and then I could decapitate
it and take out the hook at my leisure. So back to
camp we went, Euphemia picking up the little fish
as we passed, for she did not think it right to catch
fish and not eat them. They made her hands smell,
it is true; but she did not mind that when we were
camping.

I prepared the big fish (and I had a desperate time
getting the skin off), while my wife, who is one of the
daintiest cooks in the world, made the fire in the
stove and got ready the rest of the supper. She
fried the fish, because I told her that was the way
catfish ought to be cooked, although she said that it
seemed very strange to her to camp out for the sake
of one's health, and then to eat fried food.

But that fish was splendid! The very smell of it
made us hungry. Everything was good, and when
supper was over and the dishes washed, I lighted my
pipe, and we sat down under a tree to enjoy the
evening.

The sun had set behind the distant ridge ; a delightful twilight was gently subduing every color of the
scene ; the night insects were beginning to hum and
chirp ; and a fire that I had made under a tree blazed
up gayly, and threw little flakes of light into the
shadows under the shrubbery.

"Now, isn't this better than being cooped up in a
narrow, constricted house?" said I.

"Ever so much better!" said Euphemia. "Now
we know what nature is. We are sitting right down
in her lap, and she is cuddling us up. Isn't that sky

lovely! Oh, I think this is perfectly splendid!" said she, making a little dab at her face,—"if it wasn't for the mosquitoes."

"They *are* bad," I said. "I thought my pipe would keep them off, but it doesn't. There must be plenty of them down at that creek."

"Down there!" exclaimed Euphemia. "Why, there are thousands of them here! I never saw anything like it. They're getting worse every minute."

"I'll tell you what we must do," I exclaimed, jumping up. "We must make a smudge."

"What's that? do you rub it on yourself?" asked Euphemia, anxiously.

"No, it's only a great smoke. Come, let us gather up dry leaves and make a smouldering fire of them."

We managed to get up a very fair smudge, and we stood to the leeward of it until Euphemia began to cough and sneeze as if her head would come off. With tears running from her eyes, she declared that she would rather go and be eaten alive than stay in that smoke.

"Perhaps we are too near it," said I.

"That may be," she answered, "but I have had enough smoke. Why didn't I think of it before? I brought two veils! We can put these over our faces, and wear gloves."

She was always full of expedients.

Veiled and gloved, we bade defiance to the mosquitoes, and we sat and talked for half an hour or more. I made a little hole in my veil, through which I put the mouthpiece of my pipe.

When it became really dark, I lighted the lantern, and we prepared for a well-earned night's rest. The tent was spacious and comfortable, and we each had a nice little cot-bed.

"Are you going to leave the front door open all night?" said Euphemia, as I came in after a final round to see that all was right.

"I should hardly call this canvas flap a front door," I said, "but I think it would be better to leave it open; otherwise we should smother. You need not be afraid. I shall keep my gun here by my bedside, and if any one offers to come in, I'll bring him to a full stop quick enough."

"Yes, if you are awake. But I suppose we ought not to be afraid of burglars here. People in tents never are. So you needn't shut it."

It was awfully quiet and dark and lonely out there by that creek, when the light had been put out and we had gone to bed. For some reason I could not go to sleep. After I had been lying awake for an hour or two, Euphemia spoke.

"Are you awake?" said she, in a low voice, as if she were afraid of disturbing the people in the next room.

"Yes," said I. "How long have you been awake?"

"I haven't been asleep."

"Neither have I."

"Suppose we light the lantern," said she. "Don't you think it would be pleasanter?"

"It might be," I replied, "but it would draw myriads of mosquitoes. I wish I had brought a mosquito-net and a clock. It seems so lonesome without the ticking. Good night! We ought to have a long sleep, if we do much tramping about to-morrow."

In about half an hour more, just as I was beginning to be a little sleepy, she said:

"Where is that gun?"

"Here by me," I answered.

"Well, if a man should come in, try to be sure to put it up close to him before you fire. In a little tent like this the shot might scatter everywhere, if you're not careful."

"All right," I said. "Good night!"

"There's one thing we never thought of!" she presently exclaimed.

"What's that?" said I.

"Snakes," said she.

"Well, don't let's think of them. We must try to get a little sleep."

"Dear knows, I've been trying hard enough!" she said plaintively, and all was quiet again.

We succeeded this time in going to sleep, and it was broad daylight before we awoke.

That morning Old John came with our water before breakfast was ready. He also brought us some milk, as he thought we would want it. We considered this a good idea, and agreed to have him bring us a quart a day.

"Don't you want some wegetables?" said he. "I've got some nice corn and some tomatoes, and I could bring you cabbage and peas."

We had hardly expected to have fresh vegetables every day, but there seemed to be no reason why Old John should not bring them, as he had to come every day with the water and milk, and we arranged that he should furnish us daily with a few of the products of his garden.

"I could go to the butcher's and get you a steak or some chops, if you'd let me know in the mornin'," said he, intent on the profits of further commissions.

But this was going too far. We remembered we were camping out, and declined to have meat from the butcher.

John had not been gone more than ten minutes before we saw Mr. Ball approaching.

"Oh, I hope he isn't going to say we can't stay!" exclaimed Euphemia.

"How d'ye do?" said Mr. Ball, shaking hands with us. "Did you stick it out all night?"

"Oh, yes, indeed," I replied, "and expect to stick it out for many more nights, if you don't object to our occupying your land."

"No objection in the world," said he. "But it seems a little queer for people who have a good house to be livin' out here in the fields in a tent, now, doesn't it?"

"Oh, but you see," said I, and I went on and explained the whole thing to him—the advice of the doctor, the discussion about the proper place to go to, and the good reasons for fixing on this spot.

"Ye·es," said he, "that's all very well, no doubt. But how's the girl?"

"What girl?" I asked.

"Your girl. The hired girl you left at the house."

"Oh," said I. "She's always well."

"Well," said Mr. Ball, slowly turning on his heel, "if you say so, I suppose she is. But you're goin' up to the house to-day to see about her, aren't you?"

"Oh, no," said Euphemia. "We don't intend to go near the house until our camping is over."

"Just so—just so," said Mr. Ball. "I expected as much. But look here; don't you think it would be well for me to ask Dr. Ames to stop in and see how she is gettin' along? I dare say you've fixed everything for her, but that would be safer, you know. He's comin' this mornin' to vaccinate my baby, and he might stop there, just as well as not, after he has left my house."

Euphemia and I could see no necessity for this proposed visit of the doctor, but we could not well object to it, and so Mr. Ball said he would be sure and send him.

After our visitor had gone the significance of his remarks flashed on me. He still thought that Pomona was sick with something catching, and that we were afraid to stay in the house with her. But I said nothing about this to Euphemia. It would only worry her, and our vacation was to be a season of unalloyed delight.

CHAPTER X

WET BLANKETS

WE certainly enjoyed our second day in camp. All the morning, and a great part of the afternoon, we "explored." We fastened up the tent as well as we could, and then, I with my gun and Euphemia with the fishing-pole, we started up the creek. We did not go very far, for it would not do to leave the tent too long. I did not shoot anything, but Euphemia caught two or three nice little fish, and we enjoyed the sport exceedingly.

Soon after we returned in the afternoon, and while we were getting things in order for supper, we had a call from two of our neighbors, Captain Atkinson and his wife. The captain greeted us hilariously.

"Hello!" he cried. "Why, this is gay. Who would ever have thought of a domestic couple like you going on such a lark as this? We just heard about it from Old John, and we came down to see what you are up to. You've got everything very nice. I think I'd like this myself. Why, you might have a rifle-range out here. You could cut down those bushes on the other side of the creek, and put up your target over there on that hill. Then you could lie down here on the grass and bang away all day. If you'll do that I'll come down and practise with you. How long are you going to keep it up?"

I told him that we expected to spend my two weeks' vacation here.

"Not if it rains, my boy," said he. "I know what it is to camp out in the rain."

Meanwhile Mrs. Atkinson had been with Euphemia, examining the tent and our equipage generally.

"It would be very nice for a day's picnic," she said, "but I wouldn't want to stay out of doors all night."

Then, addressing me, she asked:

"Do you have to breathe the fresh air all the time, night as well as day? I expect that is a very good prescription, but I would not like to have to follow it myself."

"If the fresh air is what you must have," said the captain, "you might have got all you wanted of that without taking the trouble to come out here. You could have sat on your back porch, night and day, for the whole two weeks, and breathed all the fresh air that any man could need."

"Yes," said I, "and I might have gone down cellar and put my head in the cold-air box of the furnace. But there wouldn't have been much fun in that."

"There are a good many things that there's no fun in," said the captain. "Do you cook your own meals, or have them sent from the house?"

"Cook them ourselves, of course," said Euphemia. "We are going to have supper now. Won't you wait and take some?"

"Thank you," said Mrs. Atkinson, "but we must go."

"Yes, we must be going," said the captain. "Good-

RUDDER GRANGE

by. If it rains I'll come down after you with an umbrella."

"You need not trouble yourself about that," said I. "We shall rough it out, rain or shine."

"I'd stay here now," said Euphemia, when they had gone, "if it rained pitch."

"You mean pitchforks," I suggested.

"Yes, anything," she answered.

"Well, I don't know about the pitchforks," I said, looking over the creek at the sky, "but I am very much afraid that it is going to rain rain-water to-morrow. But that won't drive us home, will it?"

"No, indeed!" said she. "We're prepared for it. But I wish they'd stayed at home."

Sure enough, it commenced to rain that night, and we had showers all the next day. We stayed in camp during the morning, and I smoked, and we played checkers, and had a very cosey time, with a wood fire burning under a tree near by. We kept up this fire, not to dry the air, but to make things look comfortable. In the afternoon I dressed myself up in waterproof coat, boots, and hat, and started out to fish. I went down to the water and fished along the banks for an hour, but caught nothing of any consequence. This was a great disappointment, for we had expected to live on fresh fish for a great part of the time while we were camping. With plenty of fish, we could do without meat very well.

We talked the matter over on my return, and we agreed that as it seemed impossible to depend upon a supply of fish from the waters about our camp, it would be better to let Old John bring fresh meat from

110

the butcher; and as neither of us liked crackers, we also agreed that he should bring bread.

Our greatest trouble that evening was to make a fire. The wood, of which there was a good deal lying about under the trees, was now all wet and would not burn. However, we managed to get up a fire in the stove. But I did not know what we were going to do in the morning. We should have stored away some wood under shelter.

We set our little camp-table in the tent, and we had scarcely finished our supper when a very heavy rain set in, accompanied by a violent wind. The canvas at one end of our tent must have been badly fastened, for it was blown in, and in an instant our beds were deluged. I rushed out to fasten up the canvas, and got drenched almost to the skin; and although Euphemia put on her waterproof cloak as soon as she could, she was pretty wet, for the rain seemed to dash right through the tent.

This gust of wind did not last long, and the rain soon settled down into a steady drizzle, but we were in a sad plight. It was after nine o'clock before we had put things into tolerable order.

"We can't sleep in those beds," said Euphemia. "They're as wet as sop, and we shall have to go up to the house and get something to spread over them. I don't want to do it, but we mustn't catch our deaths of cold."

There was nothing to be said against this, and we prepared to start out. I would have gone by myself, but Euphemia would not consent to be left alone. It was still raining, though not very hard, and I carried an umbrella and a lantern. Climbing fences at night, with a wife, a lantern, and an umbrella to take care of, is not very agreeable, but we managed to reach the house, although once or twice we had an argument in regard to the path, which seemed to be very different at night from what it was in the daytime.

Lord Edward came bounding to the gate to meet us, and I am happy to say that he knew me at once, and wagged his tail in a very sociable way.

I had the key of a side-door in my pocket, for we had thought it wise to give ourselves command of this door, and so we let ourselves in without ringing or waking Pomona.

All was quiet within, and we went up-stairs with the lantern. Everything seemed clean and in order, and it is impossible to convey any idea of the element of comfort which seemed to pervade the house as we quietly made our way up-stairs in our wet boots and heavy, damp clothes.

The articles we wanted were in a closet, and while I was making a bundle of them Euphemia went to look for Pomona. She soon returned, walking softly.

"She's sound asleep," said she, "and I didn't think there was any need of waking her. We'll send word by John that we've been here. And oh, you can't imagine how snug and happy she did look, lying there in her comfortable bed in that nice, airy room. I'll tell you what it is, if it wasn't for the neighbors, and especially the Atkinsons, I wouldn't go back one step."

"Well," said I, "I don't know that I care so particularly about it, myself. But I suppose I couldn't stay here and leave all Thompson's things out there to take care of themselves."

"Oh, no!" said Euphemia. "And we're not going to back down. Are you ready?"

On our way down-stairs we had to pass the partly open door of our own room. I could not help holding up the lantern to look in. There was the bed, with its fair white covering and its smooth, soft pillows; there were the easy-chairs, the pretty curtains, the neat and cheerful carpet, the bureau with Euphemia's work-basket on it; there was the little table, with the book that we had been reading together turned face downward upon it; there were my slippers; there was—

"Come!" said Euphemia, "I can't bear to look in there. It's like a dead child."

And so we hurried out into the night and the rain.

We stopped at the woodshed and got an armful of dry kindling, which Euphemia was obliged to carry, as I had the bundle of bed-clothing, the umbrella, and the lantern.

Lord Edward gave a short, peculiar bark as we shut the gate behind us, but whether it was meant as a fond farewell, or a hoot of derision, I cannot say.

We found everything as we left it at the camp, and we made our beds apparently dry. But I did not sleep well. I could not help thinking that it was not safe to sleep in a bed with a substratum of wet mattress, and I worried Euphemia a little by asking her several times if she felt the dampness striking through.

To our great delight, the next day was fine and clear, and I thought I would like, better than anything else, to take Euphemia in a boat up the river, and spend the day rowing about, or resting in shady places on the shore.

But what could we do about the tent? It would be impossible to go away and leave that, with its contents, for a whole day.

When Old John came with our water, milk, bread, and a basket of vegetables, we told him of our desired excursion, and the difficulty in the way. This good man, who always had a keen scent for any advantage to himself, warmly praised the boating plan, and volunteered to send his wife and two of his younger children to stay with the tent while we were away. The old woman, he said, could do her sewing here as well as anywhere, and she would stay all day for fifty cents.

This plan pleased us, and we sent for Mrs. Old John, who came with three of her children,—all too young to leave behind, she said,—and took charge of the camp.

Our day proved to be as delightful as we had anticipated, and when we returned, hungry and tired, we were perfectly charmed to find that Mrs. Old John had our supper ready for us.

She charged a quarter extra for this service, and we did not begrudge it to her, though we declined her offer to come every day and cook and keep the place in order.

"However," said Euphemia, on second thoughts, "you may come on Saturday and clean up generally."

The next day, which was Friday, I went out in the morning with the gun. As yet I had shot nothing, for I had seen no birds about the camp which, without breaking the State laws, I thought I could kill; and so I started off up the river road.

I saw no game, but after I had walked about a mile I met a man in a wagon.

"Hello!" said he, pulling up; "you'd better be careful how you go popping around here on the public roads, frightening horses."

As I had not yet fired a single shot, I thought this was a very impudent speech, and I think so still.

"You had better wait until I begin to pop," said I, "before you make such a fuss about it."

"No," said he, "I'd rather make the fuss before you begin. My horse is skittish," and he drove off.

This man annoyed me; but as I did not, of course, wish to frighten horses, I left the road and made my way back to the tent over some very rough fields. It was a poor day for birds, and I did not get a shot.

"What a foolish man!" said Euphemia, when I told her the above incident, "to talk that way when you stood there with a gun in your hand. You might have raked his wagon, fore and aft."

That afternoon, as Euphemia and I were sitting under a tree by the tent, we were very much surprised to see Pomona come walking down the peninsula.

I was annoyed and provoked at this. We had given Pomona positive orders not to leave the place, under any pretence, while we were gone. If necessary to send for anything, she could go to the fence back of the barn, and scream across a small field to some of the numerous members of Old John's family. Under this arrangement, I felt that the house was perfectly safe.

Before she could reach us, I called out:

"Why did you leave the house, Pomona? Don't you know you should never come away and leave the house empty? I thought I had made you understand that."

"It isn't empty," said Pomona, in an entirely un-ruffled tone. "Your old boarder is there, with his wife and child."

Euphemia and I looked at each other in dismay.

"They came early this afternoon," continued Po-mona, "by the one-fourteen train, and walked up, he carrying the child."

"It can't be," cried Euphemia. "Their child's married."

"It must have married very young, then," said Pomona, "for it isn't over four years old now."

"Oh," said Euphemia, "I know! It's his grand-child."

"Grandchild!" repeated Pomona, with her coun-tenance more expressive of emotion than I had ever yet seen it.

"Yes," said Euphemia. "But how long are they going to stay? Where did you tell them we were?"

"They didn't say how long they was goin' to stay," answered Pomona. "I told them you had gone to be with some friends in the country, and that I didn't know whether you'd be home to-night or not."

"How could you tell them such a falsehood?" cried Euphemia.

"That was no falsehood," said Pomona; "it was true as truth. If you're not your own friends, I don't know who is. And I wasn't a-goin' to tell the boarder where you was till I found out whether you wanted me to do it or not. And so I left 'em and run over to Old John's, and then down here."

It was impossible to find fault with the excellent management of Pomona.

"What were they doing?" asked Euphemia.

RUDDER GRANGE

"I opened the parlor, and she was in there with the child—putting it to sleep on the sofa, I think. The boarder was out in the yard, tryin' to teach Lord Edward some tricks."

"He had better look out!" I exclaimed.

"Oh, the dog's chained and growlin' fearful! What am I to do with 'em?"

This was a difficult point to decide. If we went to see them, we might as well break up our camp, for we could not tell when we should be able to come back to it.

We discussed the matter very anxiously, and finally concluded that under the circumstances, and considering what Pomona had said about our whereabouts, it would be well for us to stay where we were and for Pomona to take charge of the visitors. If they returned to the city that evening, she was to give them a good supper before they went, sending John to the store for what was needed. If they stayed all night, she could get breakfast for them.

"We can write," said Euphemia, "and invite them to come and spend some days with us, when we are at home and everything is all right. I want dreadfully to see that child, but I don't see how I can do it now."

"No," said I. "They're sure to stay all night if we go up to the house; and then, I should have to have the tent and things hauled away, for I couldn't leave them here."

"The fact is," said Euphemia, "if we were miles away, in the woods of Maine, we couldn't leave our camp to see anybody. And this is practically the same."

"Certainly," said I; and so Pomona went away to her new charge.

117

CHAPTER XI

FOR the rest of the afternoon, and indeed far into the night, our conversation consisted almost entirely of conjectures regarding the probable condition of things at the house. We both thought we had done right, but we felt bad about it. It was not hospitable, to be sure; but then, I should have no other holiday until next year, and our friends could come at any time to see us.

The next morning Old John brought a note from Pomona. It was written with pencil on a small piece of paper torn from the margin of a newspaper, and contained the words, "Here yit."

"So you've got company," said Old John, with a smile. "That's a queer gal of yourn. She says I mustn't tell 'em you're here. As if I'd tell 'em!"

We knew well enough that Old John was not at all likely to do anything that would cut off the nice little revenue he was making out of our camp, and so we felt no concern on that score.

But we were very anxious for further news, and we told Old John to go to the house about ten o'clock and ask Pomona to send us another note.

We waited, in a very disturbed condition of mind,

118

until nearly eleven o'clock, when Old John came with a verbal message from Pomona:

"She says she's a-comin' herself as soon as she can get a chance to slip off."

This was not pleasant news. It filled our minds with a confused mass of probabilities, and it made us feel mean. How contemptible it seemed to be a party to this concealment and in league with a servant-girl who had to "slip off"!

Before long Pomona appeared, quite out of breath.

"In all my life," said she, "I never seen people like them two. I thought I was never goin' to get away."

"Are they there yet?" cried Euphemia. "How long are they going to stay?"

"Dear knows!" replied Pomona. "Their valise came up by express last night."

"Oh, we'll have to go up to the house," said Euphemia. "It won't do to stay away any longer."

"Well," said Pomona, fanning herself with her apron, "if you knowed all I know, I don't think you'd think so."

"What do you mean?" said Euphemia.

"Well, ma'am, they've just settled down and taken possession of the whole place. He says to me that he knowed you'd both want them to make themselves at home, just as if you was there, and they thought they'd better do it. He asked me did I think you would be home by Monday, and I said I didn't know, but I guessed you would. So says he to his wife, 'Won't that be a jolly lark? We'll just keep house for them here till they come.' And he says he would go down to the store and order some things if there wasn't enough in the house, and he asked her to see

119

what would be needed, which she did, and he's gone
down for 'em now. And she says that, as it was Saturday, she'd see that the house was all put to rights ;
and after breakfast she set me to sweepin' ; and it's
only by way of her dustin' the parlor and givin' me
the little girl to take for a walk that I got off at all."

"But what have you done with the child?" exclaimed Euphemia.

"Oh, I left her at Old Johnses."

"And so you think they're pleased with having the
house to themselves?" I said.

"Pleased, sir?" replied Pomona. "They're tickled
to death."

"But how do you like having strangers telling you
what to do?" asked Euphemia.

"Oh, well," said Pomona, "he's no stranger, and
she's real pleasant, and if it gives you a good camp
out, I don't mind."

Euphemia and I looked at each other. Here was
true allegiance. We would remember this.

Pomona now hurried off, and we seriously discussed
the matter, and soon came to the conclusion that
while it might be the truest hospitality to let our
friends stay at our house for a day or two and enjoy
themselves, still, it would not do for us to allow ourselves to be governed by a too delicate sentimentality.
We must go home and act our part of host and hostess.

Mrs. Old John had been at the camp ever since
breakfast-time, giving the place a Saturday cleaning.
What she had found to occupy her for so long a time
I could not imagine, but in her efforts to put in a full
half-day's work, I have no doubt she scrubbed some of
the trees. We had been so fully occupied with our

own affairs that we had paid very little attention to her, but she had probably heard pretty much all that had been said.

At noon we paid her, giving her, at her suggestion, something extra in lieu of the midday meal, which she did not stay to take, and told her to send her husband, with his wagon, as soon as possible, as we intended to break up our encampment. We determined that we would pack everything in John's wagon, and let him take the load to his house, and keep it there until Monday, when I would have the tent and accompaniments expressed to their owner. We would go home and join our friends. It would not be necessary to say where we had been.

It was hard for us to break up our camp. In many respects we had enjoyed the novel experience, and we had fully expected, during the next week, to make up for all our shortcomings and mistakes. It seemed like losing all our labor and expenditure to break up now, but there was no help for it. Our place was at home.

We did not wish to invite our friends to the camp. They would certainly have come had they known we were there, but we had no accommodations for them; neither had we any desire for even transient visitors. Besides, we both thought that we would prefer that our ex-boarder and his wife should not know that we were encamped on this little peninsula.

We set to work to pack up and get ready for moving, but the afternoon passed away without bringing Old John. Between five and six o'clock along came his oldest boy with a bucket of water.

"I'm to go back after the milk," he said.

"Hold up!" I cried. "Where is your father and his wagon? We've been waiting for him for hours."

"The horse is si—I mean he's gone to Ballville for oats."

"And why didn't he send and tell me?" I asked.

"There wasn't nobody to send," answered the boy.

"You are not telling the truth," exclaimed Euphemia. "There is always some one to send in a family like yours."

To this the boy made no answer, but again said that he would go after the milk.

"We want you to bring no milk," I cried, now quite angry. "I want you to go down to the station, and tell the driver of the express-wagon to come here immediately. Do you understand? Immediately!"

The boy declared he understood, and started off quite willingly. We did not prefer to have the express-wagon, for it was too public a conveyance, and, besides, Old John knew exactly how to do what was required. But we need not have troubled ourselves. The express-wagon did not come.

When it became dark, we saw that we could not leave that night. Even if a wagon did come, it would not be safe to drive over the fields in the darkness. And we could not go away and leave the camp equipage. I proposed that Euphemia should go up to the house, while I remained in camp. But she declined. We would keep together, whatever happened, she said.

We unpacked our cooking utensils and provisions, and had supper. There was no milk for our coffee, but we did not care. The evening did not pass gayly. We were annoyed by the conduct of Old John and the

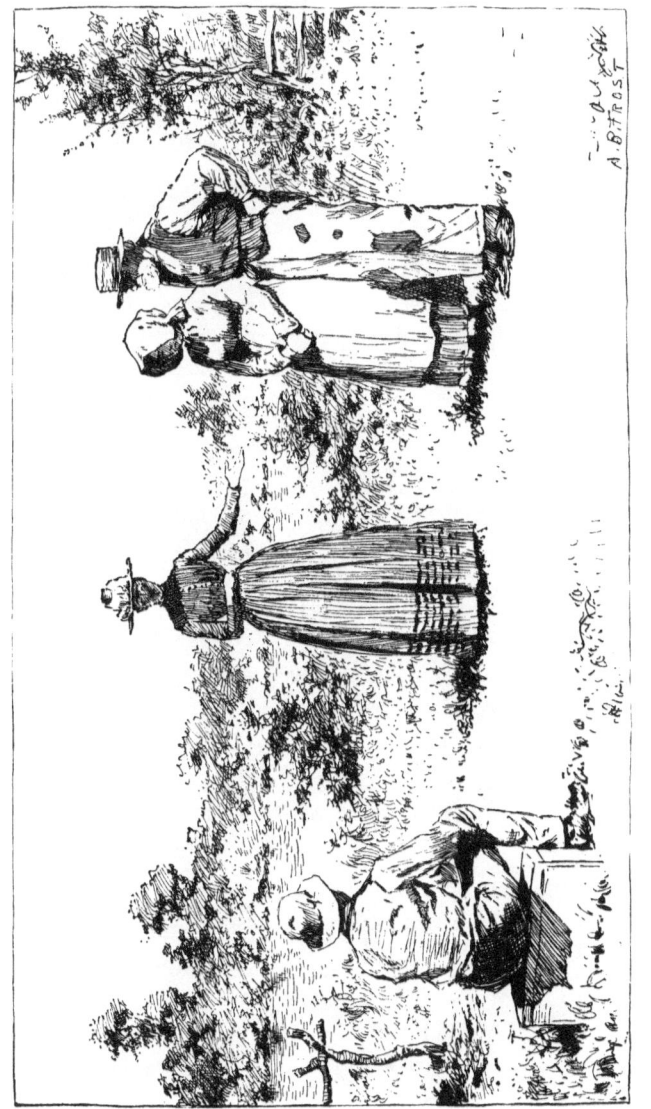

"These people have entered into a conspiracy against us."

express-man, though perhaps it was not his fault. I had given him no notice that I should need him.

And we were greatly troubled at the continuance of the secrecy and subterfuge which now had become really necessary if we did not wish to hurt our friends' feelings.

The first thing that I thought of, when I opened my eyes in the morning, was the fact that we would have to stay there all day, for we could not move on Sunday.

But Euphemia did not agree with me. After breakfast—we found that the water and the milk had been brought very early, before we were up—she stated that she did not intend to be treated in this way; she was going up to Old John's house herself, and away she went.

In less than half an hour she returned, followed by Old John and his wife, both looking much as if they had been whipped.

"These people," said she, "have entered into a conspiracy against us. I have questioned them thoroughly, and have made them answer me. The horse was at home yesterday, and the boy did not go after the express-wagon. They thought that if they could keep us here until our company had gone, we would stay as long as we originally intended, and they would continue to make money out of us. But they are mistaken. We are going home immediately."

At this point I could not help thinking that Euphemia might have consulted me in regard to her determination, but she was very much in earnest, and I would not have any discussion before these people.

"Now, listen!" said Euphemia, addressing the down-

123

cast couple. "We are going home, and you two are to stay here all this day and to-night, and take care of these things. You can't work to-day, and you can shut up your house and bring your whole family here if you choose. We will pay you for the service,— although you do not deserve a cent,—and we will leave enough here for you to eat. You must bring your own sheets and pillow-cases, and stay here until we see you on Monday morning."

Old John and his wife agreed to this plan with the greatest alacrity, apparently well pleased to get off so easily; and having locked up the smaller articles of camp furniture, we filled a valise with our personal baggage and started off home.

Our house and grounds never looked prettier than they did that morning as we stood at the gate. Lord Edward barked a welcome from his shed, and before we reached the door Pomona came running out, her face radiant.

"I'm awful glad to see you back," she said, "though I'd never have said so while you was in camp."

I patted the dog and looked into the garden. Everything was growing splendidly. Euphemia rushed to the chicken-yard. It was in first-rate order, and there were two broods of little yellow, puffy chicks.

Down on her knees went my wife, to pick up the little creatures, one by one, press their downy bodies to her cheek, and call them tootsy-wootsies; and away went I to the barn, followed by Pomona and soon afterward by Euphemia.

The cow was all right.

"I've been making butter," said Pomona, "though it don't look exactly like it ought to yet. The skim-milk I didn't know what to do with, so I gave it to Old John. He came for it every day, and was real mad once because I had given a lot of it to the dog, and couldn't let him have but a pint."

"He ought to have been mad," said I to Euphemia, as we walked up to the house. "He got ten cents a quart for that milk."

We laughed, and didn't care. We were too glad to be at home.

"But where are our friends?" I asked Pomona. We had actually forgotten them.

"Oh! they're gone out for a walk," said she. "They started off right after breakfast."

We were not sorry for this. It would be so much nicer to see our dear home again when there was nobody there but ourselves. Indoors we rushed. Our absence had been like rain on a garden. Everything now seemed fresher and brighter and more delightful. We went from room to room, and seemed to appreciate better than ever what a charming home we had.

We were so full of the delights of our return that we forgot all about the Sunday dinner and our guests; but Pomona, whom my wife was training to be an excellent cook, did not forget, and Euphemia was summoned to a consultation in the kitchen.

Dinner was late; but our guests were later. We waited as long as the state of the provisions and our appetites would permit, and then we sat down to the table and began to eat slowly. But they did not come. We finished our meal, and they were still absent. We now became quite anxious, and I proposed to Euphemia that we should go and look for them.

We started out, and our steps naturally turned toward the river. An unpleasant thought began to crowd itself into my mind, and perhaps the same thing happened to Euphemia, for, without saying anything to each other, we both turned toward the path that led to the peninsula. We crossed the field, climbed the fence, and there, in front of the tent, sat our old boarder, splitting sticks with the camp hatchet.

"Hurrah!" he cried, springing to his feet when he saw us. "How glad I am to see you back! When did you return? Isn't this splendid?"

"What?" I said, as we shook hands.

"Why, this," he cried, pointing to the tent. "Don't you see? We're camping out."

"You are!" I exclaimed, looking around for his wife, while Euphemia stood motionless, actually unable to make a remark.

"Certainly we are. It's the rarest bit of luck. My wife and Adele will be here directly. They've gone to look for water-cresses. But I must tell you how I came to make this magnificent find. We started out for a walk this morning, and we happened to hit on this place, and here we saw this gorgeous tent, with nobody near but a little tow-headed boy."

"Only a boy?" cried Euphemia.

"Yes, a young shaver of about nine or ten. I asked him what he was doing here, and he told me that this tent belonged to a gentleman who had gone away, and that he was here to watch it until he came back. Then I asked him how long the owner would probably be away, and he said he supposed for a day or two. Then a splendid idea struck me. I offered the boy a dollar to let me take his place. I knew that any sensible man would rather have me in charge of his tent than a young codger like that. The boy agreed as quick as lightning, and I paid him and sent him off. You see how little he was to be trusted! The owner of this tent will be under the greatest obligations to me. Just look at it!" he cried. "Beds, table, stove —everything anybody could want. I've camped out lots of times, but never had such a tent as this. I intended coming up this afternoon after my valise, and to tell your girl where we are. But here is my wife and little Adele."

In the midst of the salutations and the mutual surprise, Euphemia cried :

"But you don't expect to camp out now? You are coming back to our house?"

"You see," said the ex-boarder, "we should never have thought of doing anything so rude had we supposed you would have returned so soon. But your girl gave us to understand that you would not be back for days, and so we felt free to go at any time ; and I did not hesitate to make this arrangement. And now that I have really taken the responsibility of the tent and fixtures on myself, I don't think it would be right to go away and leave the place, especially as I don't know where to find that boy. The owner will be back in a day or two, and I would like to explain matters to him and give up the property in good order into his hands. And, to tell the truth, we both adore camping out, and we may never have such a chance again. We can live here splendidly. I went out to forage this morning, and found an old fellow living near by who sold me a lot of provisions,—even some coffee and sugar,—and he's to bring us some milk.

We're going to have supper in about an hour; won't you stay and take a camp meal with us? It will be a novelty for you, at any rate."

We declined this invitation, as we had so lately dined. I looked at Euphemia with a question in my eye. She understood me, and gently shook her head. It would be a shame to make any explanations which might put an end to this bit of camp life, which evidently was so eagerly enjoyed by our old friend. But we insisted that they should come up to the house and see us, and they agreed to dine with us the next evening. On Tuesday they must return to the city.

"Now, this is what I call real hospitality," said the ex-boarder, warmly grasping my hand. I could not help agreeing with him.

As we walked home I happened to look back, and saw Old John going over the fields toward the camp, carrying a little tin pail and a water-bucket.

The next day, toward evening, a storm set in, and at the hour fixed for our dinner the rain was pouring down in such torrents that we did not expect our guests. After dinner the rain ceased, and as we supposed that they might not have made any preparations for a meal, Euphemia packed up some dinner for them in a basket, and I took it down to the camp.

They were glad to see me, and said they had had a splendid time all day. They were up before sunrise, and had explored, tramped, boated, and I don't know what else.

My basket was very acceptable, and I would have

stayed awhile with them, but as they were obliged to
eat in the tent, there was no place for me to sit, it
being too wet outside, and so I soon came away.

We were in doubt whether or not to tell our friends
the true history of the camp. I thought that it was
not right to keep up the deception, while Euphemia
declared that if they were sensitive people they would
feel very badly at having broken up our plans by
their visit, and then having appropriated our camp to
themselves. She thought it would be the part of mag-
nanimity to say nothing about it.

I could not help seeing a good deal of force in her
arguments, although I wished very much to set the
thing straight, and we discussed the matter again as
we walked down to the camp after breakfast next
morning.

There we found Old John sitting on a stump. He
said nothing, but handed me a note written in lead-
pencil on a card. It was from our ex-boarder, and
informed me that early that morning he had found
that there was a tug lying in the river, which would
soon start for the city. He also found that he could
get passage on her for his party, and as this was such
a splendid chance to go home without the bother of
getting up to the station, he had just bundled his
family and his valise on board, and was very sorry
they did not have time to come up and bid us good-
by. The tent he left in charge of a very respectable
man from whom he had had supplies.

That morning I had the camp equipage packed up
and expressed to its owner. We did not care to camp
out any more that season, but thought it would be

better to spend the rest of my vacation at the sea-shore.

Our ex-boarder wrote to us that he and his wife were anxious that we should return their visit during my holidays; but as we did not see exactly how we could return a visit of the kind, we did not try to do it.

CHAPTER XII

LORD EDWARD AND THE TREE-MAN

IT was winter at Rudder Grange. The season was the same at other places, but that fact did not particularly interest Euphemia and myself. It was winter with us, and we were ready for it. That was the great point, and it made us proud to think that we had not been taken unawares, notwithstanding the many things that were to be thought of on a little farm like ours.

It is true that we had always been prepared for winter, wherever we had lived; but this was a different case. In other days it did not matter much whether we were ready or not; but now our house, our cow, our poultry, and, indeed, ourselves, might have suffered—there is no way of finding out exactly how much—if we had not made all possible preparations for the coming of cold weather.

But there was a great deal yet to be thought of and planned out, although we were ready for winter. The next thing to think of was spring.

We laid out the farm. We decided where we would have wheat, corn, potatoes, and oats. We would have a man by the day to sow and reap. The intermediate processes I thought I could attend to myself.

RUDDER GRANGE

Everything was talked over, ciphered over, and freely discussed by my wife and myself, except one matter, which I planned and worked out alone, doing most of the necessary calculations at the office, so as not to excite Euphemia's curiosity.

I had determined to buy a horse. This would be one of the most important events of our married life, and it demanded a great deal of thought, which I gave it.

The horse was chosen for me by a friend. He was an excellent beast, the horse, excelling, as my friend told me, in muscle and wit. Nothing better than this could be said about a horse. He was a sorrel animal, quite handsome, gentle enough for Euphemia to drive, and not too high-minded to do a little farm-work, if necessary. He was exactly the animal I needed.

The carriage was not quite such a success. The horse having cost a good deal more than I expected to pay, I found that I could only afford a second-hand carriage. I bought a good, serviceable vehicle which would hold four persons, if necessary, and in which there was room enough to pack parcels and baskets. It was with great satisfaction that I contemplated this feature of the carriage, which was rather a rusty-looking affair, although sound and strong enough. The harness was new, and set off the horse admirably.

On the afternoon when my purchases were completed, I did not come home by the train. I drove home in my own carriage, drawn by my own horse! The ten miles' drive was over a smooth road, and the sorrel travelled splendidly. If I had been a line of kings a mile long, all in their chariots of state, with gold and silver, and outriders, and music, and banners waving in the wind, I could not have been prouder than when I drew up in front of my house.

There was a wagon-gate at one side of the front fence, which had never been used except by the men who brought coal; and I got out and opened this, very quietly, so as not to attract the attention of Euphemia. It was earlier than I usually returned, and she would not be expecting me. I was then about to lead the horse up a somewhat grass-grown carriageway to the front door, but I reflected that Euphemia might be looking out of some of the windows, and I would better drive up. So I got in and drove very slowly to the door.

However, she heard the unaccustomed noise of wheels, and looked out of the parlor window. She did not see me, but immediately came around to the door. I hurried out of the carriage so quickly that, not being familiar with the steps, I barely escaped tripping.

When she opened the front door she was surprised to see me standing by the horse.

"Have you hired a carriage?" she cried. "Are we going to ride?"

"My dear," said I, as I took her by the hand, "we are going to ride. But I have not hired a carriage. I have bought one. Do you see this horse? He is ours—our own horse."

If you could have seen the face that was turned up to me—all you other men in the world—you would have torn your hair in despair.

Afterward she went around and around that horse; she patted his smooth sides; she looked with admiration at his strong, well-formed legs; she stroked his head; she smoothed his mane; she was brimful of joy.

When I had brought the horse some water in a bucket—and what a pleasure it was to water one's own horse!—Euphemia rushed into the house and got her hat and cloak, and we took a little drive.

I doubt if any horse ever drew two happier people. Euphemia said but little about the carriage. That was a necessary adjunct, and it was good enough for the present. But the horse! How nobly and with what vigor he pulled us up the hills, and how carefully and strongly he held the carriage back as we went down! How easily he trotted over the level road, caring nothing for the ten miles he had gone that afternoon! What a sensation of power it gave us to think that all that strength and speed and endurance was ours, that it would go where we wished, that it would wait for us as long as we chose, that it was at our service day and night—that it was a horse, and we owned it!

When we returned, Pomona saw us come in,—she had not known of our drive,—and when she heard the news she was as wild with proud delight as anybody. She wanted to unharness him, but this I could not allow. We did not wish to be selfish, but after she had seen and heard what we thought was enough for her, we were obliged to send her back to the kitchen for the sake of the dinner.

Then we unharnessed him. I say we, for Euphemia stood by and I explained everything, for some day, she said, she might want to do it herself. Then I led him into the stable. How nobly he trod, and how finely his hoofs sounded on the stable floor!

There was hay in the mow, and I had brought a bag of oats under the seat of the carriage.

"Isn't it just delightful," said Euphemia, "that we haven't any man? If we had a man he would take the horse at the door, and we should be deprived of all this. It wouldn't be half like owning a horse."

In the morning I drove down to the station, Euphemia by my side. She drove back, and Old John came up and attended to the horse. This he was to do, for the present, for a small stipend. In the afternoon Euphemia came down after me. How I enjoyed those drives! Before this I had thought it ever so much more pleasant and healthful to walk to and from the station than to ride, but then I did not own a horse. At night I attended to everything, Euphemia generally following me about the stable with a lantern. When the days grew longer we would have delightful drives after dinner, and even now we planned to have early breakfasts, and go to the station by the longest possible way.

One day in the following spring I was coming home from the station with Euphemia,—we seldom took pleasure drives now, we were so busy on the place,— and as we reached the house I heard the dog barking savagely. He was loose in the little orchard by the side of the house. As I drove in, Pomona came running to the carriage.

"Man up the tree!" she shouted.

I helped Euphemia out, left the horse standing by the door, and ran to the dog, followed by my wife and Pomona. There really was a man up the tree, and Lord Edward was doing his best to get at him, springing wildly at the tree and fairly shaking with rage.

I looked up at the man. He was a thoroughbred tramp, burly, dirty, generally unkempt; but, unlike most tramps, he looked very much frightened. His position, on a high crotch of an apple-tree, was not altogether comfortable, and although, for the present, it was safe, the fellow seemed to have a wavering faith in the strength of apple-tree branches, and the moment he saw me, he earnestly besought me to take that dog away and let him down.

I made no answer, but turning to Pomona, I asked her what all this meant.

"Why, sir, you see," said she, "I was in the kitchen bakin' pies, and this fellow must have got over the fence at the side of the house, for the dog didn't see him, and the first thing I knowed he was stickin' his head in the window, and he asked me to give him somethin' to eat. And when I said I'd see in a minute if there was anything for him, he says to me, 'Gimme a piece of one of them pies'—pies I'd just baked and was settin' to cool on the kitchen table ! 'No, sir,' says I, 'I'm not goin' to cut one of them pies for you, or any one like you.' 'All right !' says he. 'I'll come in and help myself.' He must have known there was no man about, and comin' the way he did, he hadn't seen the dog. So he come round to the kitchen door ; but I shot out before he got there and unchained Lord Edward. I guess he saw the dog when he got to the door, and at any rate he heard the chain clankin', and he didn't go in, but just put for the gate. But Lord Edward was after him so quick that he hadn't no time to go to no gates. It was all he could do to scoot up this tree, and if he'd been a millionth part of a minute later he'd 'a' been in another world by this time."

I looked up at the man.

RUDDER GRANGE

The man, who had not attempted to interrupt Pomona's speech, now began again to implore me to let him down, while Euphemia looked pitifully at him, and was about, I think, to intercede with me in his favor, but my attention was drawn off from her by the strange conduct of the dog. Believing, I suppose, that he might leave the tramp for a moment, now that I had arrived, he had dashed away to another tree, where he was barking furiously, standing on his hind legs and clawing at the trunk.

"What's the matter over there?" I asked.

"Oh, that's the other fellow," said Pomona. "He's no harm." And then, as the tramp made a movement as if he would try to come down and make a rush for safety during the absence of the dog, she called out, "Here, boy! here, boy!" and in an instant Lord Edward was again raging at his post at the foot of the apple-tree.

I was grievously puzzled by all this, and walked over to the other tree, followed, as before, by Euphemia and Pomona.

"This one," said the latter, "is a tree-man—"

"I should think so," said I, as I caught sight of a person in gray trousers standing among the branches of a cherry-tree not very far from the kitchen door. The tree was not a large one, and the branches were not strong enough to allow him to sit down on them, although they supported him well enough, as he stood close to the trunk just out of reach of Lord Edward.

"This is a very unpleasant position, sir," said he, when I reached the tree. "I simply came into your yard on a matter of business, and finding that raging beast attacking a person in a tree, I had barely time

137

RUDDER GRANGE

to get up into this tree myself before he dashed at
me.   Luckily I was out of his reach ; but I very much
fear I have lost some of my property."

"No, he hasn't," said Pomona.   "It was a big book
he dropped.   I picked it up and took it into the
house.   It's full of pictures of pears and peaches and
flowers.   I've been lookin' at it.   That's how I knew
what he was.   And there was no call for his gittin' up
a tree.   Lord Edward never would have gone after
him if he hadn't run as if he had guilt on his soul."

"I suppose, then," said I, addressing the individual
in the cherry-tree, "that you came here to sell me
some trees."

"Yes, sir," said he, quickly, "trees, shrubs, vines,
evergreens—everything suitable for a gentleman's
country villa.   I can sell you something quite remarkable, sir, in the way cf cherry-trees—French
ones, just imported ; bear fruit three times the size of
anything that could be produced on a tree like this.
And pears—fruit of the finest flavor and enormous
size—"

"Yes," said Pomona.   "I seen them in the book.
But they must grow on a ground-vine.   No tree
couldn't hold such pears as them."

Here Euphemia reproved Pomona's forwardness,
and I invited the tree-agent to get down out of the
tree.

"Thank you," said he, "but not while that dog is
loose.   If you will kindly chain him up, I will get my
book and show you specimens of some of the finest
small fruit in the world, all imported from the first
nurseries of Europe—the Red-gold Amber Muscat
grape, the—"

"Oh, please let him down!" said Euphemia, her eyes beginning to sparkle.

I slowly walked toward the tramp-tree, revolving various matters in my mind. We had not spent much money on the place during the winter, and we now had a small sum which we intended to use for the advantage of the farm, but had not yet decided what to do with it. It behooved me to be careful.

I told Pomona to run and get me the dog-chain, and I stood under the tree, listening, as well as I could, to the tree-agent talking to Euphemia, and paying no attention to the impassioned entreaties of the tramp in the crotch above me. When the chain was brought, I hooked one end of it in Lord Edward's collar, and then I took a firm grasp of the other. Telling Pomona to bring the tree-agent's book from the house, I called to that individual to get down from his tree. He promptly obeyed, and, taking the book from Pomona, began to show the pictures to Euphemia.

"You had better hurry, sir," I called out. "I can't hold this dog very long." And, indeed, Lord Edward had made a run toward the agent which jerked me very forcibly in his direction. But a movement by the tramp had quickly brought the dog back to his more desired victim.

"If you will just tie up that dog, sir," said the agent, "and come this way, I would like to show you the Meltinagua pear—dissolves in the mouth like snow, sir; trees will bear next year."

"Oh, come look at the Royal Sparkling Ruby grape!" cried Euphemia. "It glows in the sun like a gem."

"Yes," said the agent, "and fills the air with fragrance during the whole month of September—"

"I tell you," I shouted, "I can't hold this dog another minute! The chain is cutting the skin off my hands. Run, sir, run! I'm going to let go!"

"Run! run!" cried Pomona. "Fly for your life!"

The agent now began to be frightened, and shut up his book.

"If you only could see the plates, sir, I'm sure—"

"Are you ready?" I cried, as the dog, excited by Pomona's wild shouts, made a bolt in his direction.

"Good day, if I must," said the agent, as he hurried to the gate. But there he stopped.

"There is nothing, sir," he said, "that would so improve your place as a row of the Spitzenberg Sweet-scented Balsam fir along this fence. I'll sell you three-year-old trees—"

"He's loose! ' I shouted, as I dropped the chain.

In a second the agent was on the other side of the gate. Lord Edward made a dash toward him, but, stopping suddenly, flew back to the tree of the tramp

"If you should conclude, sir," said the tree-agent, looking over the fence, "to have a row of those firs along here—"

"My good sir," said I, "there is no row of firs there now, and the fence is not very high. My dog, as you see, is very much excited, and I cannot answer for the consequences if he takes it into his head to jump over."

The tree-agent turned and walked slowly away.

"Now, look-a-here," cried the tramp from the tree, in the voice of a very ill-used person, "ain't you goin' to fasten up that dog and let me git down?"

I walked up close to the tree and addressed him.

"No," said I, "I am not. When a man comes to my place, bullies a young girl who is about to relieve his hunger, and then boldly determines to enter my house and help himself to my property, I don't propose to fasten up any dog that may happen to be after him. If I had another dog, I'd let him loose, and give this faithful beast a rest. You can do as you please. You can come down and have it out with the dog, or you can stay up there until I have had my dinner. Then I will drive down to the village and bring up the constable and deliver you into his hands. We want no such fellows as you about."

With that, I unhooked the chain from Lord Edward, and walked off to put up the horse. The man shouted after me, but I paid no attention. I did not feel in a good humor with him.

Euphemia was much disturbed by the various occurrences of the afternoon. She was sorry for the man in the tree; she was sorry that the agent for the Royal Ruby grape had been obliged to go away; and I had a good deal of trouble during dinner to make her see things in the proper light. But I succeeded at last.

I did not hurry through dinner, and when we had finished I went to my work at the barn. Tramps are not generally pressed for time, and Pomona had been told to give our captive something to eat.

I was just locking the door of the carriage-house when Pomona came running to me to tell me that the tramp wanted to see me about something very important—just a minute, he said. I put the key in my pocket and walked over to the tree. It was now

141

RUDDER GRANGE

almost dark, but I could see that the dog, the tramp, and the tree still kept their respective places.

"Look-a-here," said the individual in the crotch, "you don't know how dreadful oneasy these limbs gits after you've been settin' up here as long as I have. And I don't want to have nuthin' to do with no constables. I'll tell you what I'll do : if you'll chain up that dog and let me go, I'll fix things so that you'll not be troubled no more by no tramps."

"How will you do that?" I asked.

"Oh, never you mind," said he. "I'll give you my word of honor I'll do it. There's a reg'lar understandin' among us fellers, you know."

I considered the matter. The word of honor of a fellow such as he was could not be worth much, but the merest chance of getting rid of tramps should not be neglected. I went in to talk to Euphemia about it, although I knew what she would say. I reasoned with myself as much as with her.

"If we put this one fellow in prison for a few weeks," I said, "the benefit is not very great. If we are freed from all tramps for the season, the benefit is very great. Shall we try for the greatest good?"

"Certainly," said Euphemia ; "and his legs must be dreadfully stiff."

So I went out, and after a struggle of some minutes I chained Lord Edward to a post at a little distance from the apple-tree. When he was secure, the tramp descended nimbly from his perch, notwithstanding his stiff legs, and hurried out of the gate. He stopped to make no remarks over the fence. With a wild howl of disappointed ambition, Lord Edward threw himself after him. But the chain held.

142

RUDDER GRANGE

A lane of moderate length led from our house to the main road, and the next day, as we were riding home, I noticed on the trunk of a large tree which stood at the corner of the lane and road a curious mark. I drew up to see what it was, but we could not make it out. It was a very rude device, cut deeply into the tree, and somewhat resembled a square, a circle, a triangle, and a cross, with some smaller marks beneath it. I felt sure that our tramp had cut it, and that it had some significance which would be understood by the members of his fraternity.

And it must have had, for no tramps came near us all that summer. We were visited by a needy person now and then, but by no member of the regular army of tramps.

One afternoon, that fall, I walked home, and at the corner of the lane I saw a tramp looking up at the mark on the tree, which was still quite distinct.

"What does that mean?" I said, stepping up to him.

"How do I know?" said the man, "and what do you want to know fur?"

"Just out of curiosity," I said. "I have often noticed it. I think you can tell me what it means, and if you will do so I'll give you a dollar."

"And keep mum about it?" said the man.

"Yes," I replied, taking out the dollar."

"All right!" said the tramp. "That sign means that the man that lives up this lane is a mean, stingy cuss, with a wicked dog, and it's no good to go there."

I handed him the dollar and went away, perfectly satisfied with my reputation.

I wish here to make some mention of Euphemia's

methods of work in her chicken-yard. She kept a book, which she at first called her "Fowl Record," but she afterward changed the name to "Poultry Register." I never could thoroughly understand this book, although she has often explained every part of it to me. She had pages for registering the age, description, time of purchase or of birth, and subsequent performances of every fowl in her yard. She had divisions of the book for expenses, profits, probable losses and positive losses. She noted the number of eggs put under each setting hen, the number of eggs cracked per day, the number spoiled, and, finally, the number hatched. Each chick, on emerging from its shell, was registered, and an account kept of its subsequent life and adventures. There were frequent calculations regarding the advantages of various methods of treatment, and there were statements of the results of a great many experiments—something like this: "Set Toppy and her sister Pinky, April 2, 187–; Toppy with twelve eggs—three Brahma, four common, and five Leghorn; Pinky with thirteen eggs (as she weighs four ounces more than her sister), of which three were Leghorn, five common, and five Brahma. During the 22d and 23d of April (same year) Toppy hatched out four Brahmas, two commons, and three Leghorns, while her sister, on these days and the morning of the day following, hatched two Leghorns, six commons, and only one Brahma. Now, could Toppy, who had only three Brahma eggs and hatched out four of that breed, have exchanged eggs with her sister, thus making it possible for her to hatch out six common chickens when she only had five eggs of that kind? Or did the eggs get mixed up in some way before

144

going into the possession of the hens? Look into probabilities."

These probabilities must have puzzled Euphemia a great deal, but they never disturbed her equanimity. She was always as tranquil and good-humored about her poultry-yard as if every hen laid an egg every day, and a hen-chick was hatched out of every egg.

For it may be remembered that the principle underlying Euphemia's management of her poultry was what might be designated as the "cumulative hatch." That is, she wished every chicken hatched in her yard to become the mother of a brood of her own during the year, and every one of this brood to raise another brood the next year, and so on, in a kind of geometrical progression. This plan called for a great many mother fowls, and so Euphemia based her highest hopes on a great annual preponderance of hens.

We ate a good many young roosters that fall, for Euphemia would not allow all the products of her yard to go to market, and, also, a great many eggs and fowls were sold. She had not contented herself with her original stock of poultry, but had bought fowls during the winter, and she certainly had extraordinary good luck, or else her extraordinary system worked extraordinarily well.

CHAPTER XIII

POMONA'S NOVEL

It was in the latter part of August of that year that it became necessary for some one in the office in which I was engaged to go to St. Louis to attend to important business. Everything seemed to point to me as the fit person, for I understood the particular business better than any one else. I felt that I ought to go, but I did not altogether like to do it. I went home, and Euphemia and I talked over the matter far into the regulation sleeping-hours.

There were very good reasons why we should go, for of course I would not think of taking such a journey without Euphemia. In the first place, it would be of advantage to me, in my business connection, to take the trip, and then, it would be such a charming journey for us. We had never been west of the Alleghanies, and nearly all the country we would see would be new to us. We could come home by the Great Lakes and Niagara, and the prospect was delightful to both of us. But then, we would have to leave Rudder Grange for at least three weeks, and how could we do that?

This was indeed a difficult question to answer. Who could take care of our garden, our poultry, our

horse and cow, and all their complicated belongings?
The garden was in admirable condition. Our vegetables were coming in every day in just that fresh and
satisfactory condition—altogether unknown to people
who buy vegetables—for which I had labored so faith-
fully, and about which I had had so many cheerful
anticipations. As to Euphemia's chicken-yard with
Euphemia away—the subject was too great for us.
We did not even discuss it. But we would give up
all the pleasures of our home for the chance of this
most desirable excursion, if we could but think of
some one who would come and take care of the place
while we were gone. Rudder Grange could not run
itself for three weeks.

We thought of every available person. Old John
would not do. We did not feel that we could trust
him. We thought of several of our friends ; but there
was, in both our minds, a certain shrinking from the
idea of handing over the place to any of them for such
a length of time. For my part, I said, I would rather
leave Pomona in charge than any one else ; but then,
Pomona was young and a girl. Euphemia agreed with
me that she would rather trust her than any one else,
but she also agreed in regard to the disqualifications.
So when I went to the office the next morning we
had fully determined to go on the trip if we could
find some one to take charge of our place while we
were gone. When I returned from the office in the
afternoon I had agreed to go to St. Louis. By this
time I had no choice in the matter, unless I wished
to interfere very much with my own interests. We
were to start in two days. If in that time we could
get any one to stay at the place, very well ; if not,

Pomona must assume the charge. We were not able to get any one, and Pomona did assume the charge. It is surprising how greatly relieved we felt when we were obliged to come to this conclusion. The arrangement was exactly what we wanted, and now that there was no help for it, our consciences were easy.

We felt sure that there would be no danger to Pomona. Lord Edward would be with her, and she was a young person who was extraordinarily well able to take care of herself. Old John would be within call in case she needed him, and I borrowed a bull-dog to be kept in the house at night. Pomona herself was more than satisfied with the plan.

We made out, the night before we left, a long and minute series of directions for her guidance in household, garden, and farm matters, and directed her to keep a careful record of everything noteworthy that might occur. She was fully supplied with all the necessaries of life, and it has seldom happened that a young girl has been left in such a responsible and independent position as that in which we left Pomona. She was very proud of it.

Our journey was ten times more delightful than we had expected it would be, and successful in every way; yet, although we enjoyed every hour of the trip, we were no sooner fairly on our way home than we became so wildly anxious to get there that we reached Rudder Grange on Wednesday, whereas we had written that we would be home on Thursday. We arrived early in the afternoon, and walked up from the station, leaving our baggage to be sent in the express-wagon. As we approached our dear home, we wanted to run, we were so eager to see it.

RUDDER GRANGE

There it was, the same as ever. I lifted the gate-latch; the gate was locked. We ran to the carriage-gate; that was locked, too. Just then I noticed a placard on the fence; it was not printed, but the lettering was large, apparently made with ink and a brush. It read:

TO BE SOLD

FOR TAXES

We stood and looked at each other. Euphemia turned pale.

"What does this mean?" said I. "Has our landlord—"

I could say no more. The dreadful thought arose that the place might pass away from us. We were not yet ready to buy it. But I did not put the thought in words. There was a field next to our lot, and I got over the fence and helped Euphemia over.

Then we climbed our side-fence. This was more difficult, but we accomplished it without thinking much about its difficulties; our hearts were too full of painful apprehensions. I hurried to the front door; it was locked. All the lower windows were shut. We went around to the kitchen. What surprised us more than anything else was the absence of Lord Edward. Had *he* been sold?

Before we reached the back part of the house, Euphemia said she felt faint and must sit down. I led her to a tree near by, under which I had made a rustic chair. The chair was gone. She sat on the grass, and I ran to the pump for some water. I looked for the bright tin dipper which always hung by the pump. It was not there. But I had a travelling-cup

149

in my pocket, and as I was taking it out I looked around me. There was an air of bareness over everything. I did not know what it all meant, but I know that my hand trembled as I took hold of the pump-handle and began to pump.

At the first sound of the pump-handle I heard a deep bark in the direction of the barn, and then furiously around the corner came Lord Edward. Before I had filled the cup he was bounding about me. I believe the glad welcome of the dog did more to revive Euphemia than the water. He was delighted to see us, and in a moment up came Pomona, running from the barn. Her face was radiant, too. We felt relieved. Here were two friends who looked as if they were neither sold nor ruined.

Pomona quickly saw that we were ill at ease, and before I could put a question to her she divined the cause. Her countenance fell.

"You know," said she, "you said you wasn't comin' till to-morrow. If you only *had* come then—I was goin' to have everything just exactly right—an' now you had to climb in—"

And the poor girl looked as if she might cry, which would have been a wonderful thing for Pomona to do.

"Tell me one thing," said I. "What about—those taxes?"

"Oh, that's all right," she cried. "Don't think another minute about that. I'll tell you all about it soon. But come in first, and I'll get you some lunch in a minute."

We were somewhat relieved by Pomona's statement that it was "all right" in regard to the tax-poster, but we were very anxious to know all about the matter. Pomona, however, gave us little chance to ask her any questions. As soon as she had made ready our lunch, she asked us, as a particular favor, to give her three-quarters of an hour to herself. "And then," said she, "I'll have everything looking just as if it was to-morrow."

We respected her feelings, for of course it was a great disappointment to her to be taken thus unawares, and we remained in the dining-room until she appeared and announced that she was ready for us to go about. We availed ourselves quickly of the privilege, and Euphemia hurried to the chicken-yard, while I bent my steps toward the garden and barn. As I went out I noticed that the rustic chair was in its place, and passing the pump I looked for the dipper. It was there. I asked Pomona about the chair, but she did not answer as quickly as was her habit.

"Would you rather," said she, "hear it all together, when you come in, or have it in little bits, head and tail, all of a jumble?"

I called to Euphemia and asked her what she thought, and she was so anxious to get to her chickens that she said she would much rather wait and hear it all together. We found everything in perfect order —the garden was even free from weeds, a thing I had not expected. If it had not been for that cloud on the front fence I should have been happy enough. Pomona had said it was all right, but she could not have paid the taxes—however, I would wait; and I went to the barn.

When Euphemia came in from the poultry-yard she called me and said she was in a hurry to hear Pomona's account of things. So I went in, and we sat on the

side-porch, where it was shady, while **Pomona**, producing some sheets of foolscap paper, took **her seat** on
the upper step

"I wrote down the things of any account that happened," said she, "as you told me to, and while I was
about it I thought I'd make it like a novel. It would
be jus' as true, and p'r'aps more amusin'. I suppose
you don't mind?"

No, we did not mind. So she went on:

"I haven't got no name for my novel. I intended
to think one out to-night. I wrote this all of nights.
And I don't read the first chapters, for they tell about
my birth and my parentage and my early adventures.
I'll just come down to what happened to me while
you was away, because you'll be more anxious to hear
about that. All that's written here is true, jus' the
same as if I told it to you, but I've put it into
novel language because it seems to come easier to
me."

And then, in a voice somewhat different from her
ordinary tones, as if the "novel language" demanded
it, she began to read:

"Chapter Five. The Lonely house and the Faithful
friend. Thus was I left alone. None but two dogs to
keep me com-pa-ny. I milk-ed the lowing kine and
water-ed and fed the steed, and then, after my fru-gal
repast, I clos-ed the man-si-on, shutting out all re-
collections of the past and also foresights into the
future. That night was a me-mor-able one. I slept
soundly until the break of morn, but had the events
transpired which afterwards occur-red, what would
have hap-pen-ed to me no tongue can tell. Early the
next day nothing hap-pen-ed. Soon after breakfast,

the vener-able John came to bor-row some ker-o-sene oil and a half a pound of sugar, but his attempt was foil-ed. I knew too well the in-sid-i-ous foe. In the very out-set of his vil-li-an-y I sent him home with an empty can. For two long days I wander-ed amid the ver-dant pathways of the gar-den and to the barn, whenever and anon my du-ty call-ed me, nor did I e'er neg-lect the fowlery. No cloud o'er-spread this happy pe-ri-od of my life. But the cloud was ri-sing in the hori-zon although I saw it not.

"It was about twenty-five minutes after eleven, on the morning of a Thursday, that I sat pondering in my mind the ques-ti-on what to do with the butter and the veg-et-ables. Here was butter, and here was green corn and lima-beans and trophy tomats, far more than I e'er could use. And here was a horse, idly cropping the fol-i-age in the field, for as my em-ployer had advis-ed and order-ed I had put the steed to grass. And here was a wagon, none too new, which, had it the top taken off, or even the curtains roll-ed up, would do for a li-cen-sed vender. With the truck and butter, and mayhap some milk, I could load that wagon—"

"Oh, Pomona," interrupted Euphemia, "you don't mean to say that you were thinking of doing anything like that?"

"Well, I was just beginnin' to think of it," said Pomona, "but of course I couldn't have gone away and left the house. And you'll see I didn't do it." And then she continued her novel: "But while my thoughts were thus employ-ed, I heard Lord Edward burst into bark-ter—"

At this Euphemia and I could not help bursting

153

into laughter. Pomona did not seem at all confused, but went on with her reading :

"I hurried to the door, and, look-ing out, I saw a wagon at the gate. Re-pair-ing there, I saw a man. Said he, 'Wilt open this gate?' I had fas-ten-ed up the gates and remov-ed every steal-able ar-ticle from the yard."

Euphemia and I looked at each other. This ex-plained the absence of the rustic seat and the dipper.

"Thus, with my mind at ease, I could let my faith-ful fri-end, the dog, for he it was, roam with me through the grounds, while the fi-erce bull-dog guard-ed the man-si-on within. Then said I, quite bold, unto him, 'No ; I let in no man here. My em-ploy-er and em-ploy-er-ess are now from home. What do you want?' Then says he, as bold as brass, 'I've come to put the light-en-ing rods upon the house. Open the gate.' 'What rods?' says I. 'The rods as was order-ed,' says he, 'open the gate.' I stood and gaz-ed at him. Full well I saw through his pinch-beck mask. I knew his tricks. In the ab-sence of my em-ploy-er, he would put up rods, and ever so many more than was wanted, and likely, too, some miser-able trash that would attrack the light-en-ing, instead of keep-ing it off. Then, as it would spoil the house to take them down, they would be kept, and pay de-mand-ed. 'No, sir,' says I. 'No light-en-ing rods upon this house whilst I stand here,' and with that I walk-ed away, and let Lord Edward loose. The man he storm-ed with pas-si-on. His eyes flash-ed fire. He would e'en have scal-ed the gate, but when he saw the dog he did forbear. As it was then near noon, I strode away to feed the fowls ; but when I did return, I saw a sight which froze the blood with-in my veins—"

"The dog didn't kill him?" cried Euphemia.

"Oh, no, ma'am!" said Pomona. "You'll see that that wasn't it. At one corn-er of the lot, in front, a base boy, who had accompa-ni-ed this man, was bang-ing on the fence with a long stick, and thus attrack-ing to hisself the rage of Lord Edward, while the vile intrig-er of a light-en-ing rod-der had brought a lad-der to the other side of the house, up which he had now as-cend-ed, and was on the roof. What horrors fill-ed my soul! How my form trembl-ed! This," continued Pomona, "is the end of the novel;" and she laid her foolscap pages on the porch.

Euphemia and I exclaimed, with one voice, against this. We had just reached the most exciting part, and, I added, we had heard nothing yet about that affair of the taxes.

"You see, sir," said Pomona, "it took me so long to write out the chapters about my birth, my parentage, and my early adventures, that I hadn't time to finish up the rest. But I can tell you what happened after that jus' as well as if I had writ it out." And so she went on, much more glibly than before, with the ac-count of the doings of the lightning-rod man.

"There was that wretch on top of the house, a-fixin' his old rods an' hammerin' away for dear life. He'd brought his ladder over the side-fence, where the dog, a-barkin' an' plungin' at the boy outside, couldn't see him. I stood dumb for a minute, an' then I knowed I had him. I rushed into the house, got a piece of well-rope, tied it to the bull-dog's collar, an' dragged him out an' fastened him to the bottom rung of the ladder. Then I walks over to the front fence with Lord Edward's chain, for I knew that if he got at that bull-dog there'd be times, for they'd never been allowed to see each other yet. So says I to the boy, 'I'm goin' to tie up the dog, so you needn't be afraid of his jumpin' over the fence'—which he couldn't do, or the boy would have been a corpse for twenty minutes, or maybe half an hour. The boy kinder laughed, an' said I needn't mind, which I didn't. Then I went to the gate, an' I clicked to the horse which was standin' there, an' off he starts, as good as gold, an' trots down the road. The boy he said somethin' or other pretty bad, an' away he goes after him ; but the horse was a-trottin' real fast, an' had a good start."

"How on earth could you ever think of doing such things?" said Euphemia. "That horse might have upset the wagon and broken all the lightning-rods, besides running over I don't know how many people."

"But you see, ma'am, that wasn't my lookout," said Pomona. "I was a-defendin' the house, an' the enemy must expect to have things happen to him. So then I hears an awful row on the roof, an' there was the man just coming down the ladder. He'd heard the horse go off, an' when he got about half-way down, an' caught a sight of the bull-dog, he was madder than ever you seed a lightnin'-rodder in all your born days. 'Take that dog off of there!' he yelled at me. 'No, I won't,' says I. 'I never see a girl like you since I was born!' he screams at me. 'I guess it would 'a' been better fur you if you had,' says I. An' then he was so mad he couldn't stand it any longer, an' he comes down as low as he could, an'

"Take that dog off of there!"

when he saw just how long the rope was,—which was pretty short,—he made a jump, an' landed clear of the dog. Then he went on dreadful because he couldn't get at his ladder to take it away ; an' I wouldn't untie the dog, because if I had he'd 'a' torn the tendons out of that fellow's legs in no time. I never see a dog in such a boiling passion, an' yet never making no sound at all but blood-curdlin' grunts. An' I don't see how the rodder would 'a' got his ladder at all if the dog hadn't made an awful jump at him, an' jerked the ladder down. It just missed your geranium-bed, an' the rodder he ran to the other end of it, an' began pullin' it away, dog an' all. 'Look-a-here,' says I, 'we can fix him now.' An' so he cooled down enough to help me, an' I unlocked the front door, an' we pushed the bottom end of the ladder in, dog an' all; an' then I shut the door as tight as it would go, an' untied the end of the rope, an' the rodder pulled the ladder out while I held the door to keep the dog from follerin', which he came pretty near doin', anyway. But I locked him in, an' then the man began stormin' again about his wagon ; but when he looked out an' see the boy comin' back with it,—for somebody must 'a' stopped the horse,— he stopped stormin' an' went to put up his ladder ag'in. 'No, you don't,' says I. 'I'll let the big dog loose next time, an' if I put him at the foot of your ladder you'll never come down.' 'But I want to go an' take down what I put up,' he says ; 'I ain't a-goin' on with this job.' 'No,' says I, 'you ain't; an' you can't go up there to wrench off them rods an' make rain-holes in the roof, neither.' He couldn't get no madder than he was then, an' fur a minute or two he couldn't speak; an' then he says, 'I'll have satisfaction for this.' An' says I, 'How?' An' says he, 'You'll see what it is to interfere with a ordered job.' An' says I, 'There wasn't no order about it.' An' says he, 'I'll show you better than that;' an' he goes to his wagon an' gits a book. 'There,' says he, 'read that.' 'What of it?' says I. 'There's nobody of the name of Ball lives here.' That took the man kinder aback, an' he said he was told it was the only house on the lane; which I said was right, only it was the next lane he oughter 'a' gone to. He said no more after that, but just put his ladder in his wagon an' went off. But I was not altogether rid of him. He left a trail of his baleful presence behind him.

"That horrid bull-dog wouldn't let me come into the house! No matter what door I tried, there he was, just foamin' mad. I let him stay till nearly night, an' then went an' spoke kind to him; but it was no good. He'd got an awful spite ag'in' me. I found something to eat down cellar, an' I made a fire outside an' roasted some corn an' potatoes. That night I slep' in the barn. I wasn't afraid to be away from the house, for I knew it was safe enough with that dog in it an' Lord Edward outside. For three days, Sunday an' all, I was kep' out of this here house. I got along pretty well with the sleepin' an' the eatin', but the drinkin' was the worst. I couldn't get no coffee or tea; but there was plenty of milk."

"Why didn't you get some man to come and attend to the dog?" I asked. "It was dreadful to live that way."

"Well, I didn't know no man that could do it," said Pomona. "The dog would 'a' been too much for Old

John, an' besides, he was mad about the kerosene. Sunday afternoon Captain Atkinson an' Mrs. Atkinson an' their little girl in a push-wagon come here, an' I told 'em you was gone away; but they says they would stop a minute, an' could I give them a drink. An' I had nothin' to give it to them but an old chicken-bowl that I had washed out, for even the dipper was in the house; an' I told 'em everything was locked up, which was true enough, though they must 'a' thought you was a queer kind of people; but I wasn't a-goin' to say nothin' about the dog, fur, to tell the truth, I was ashamed to do it. So as soon as they'd gone, I went down into the cellar,—it's lucky that I had the key for the ouside cellar door,—an' I got a piece of fat corn-beef an' the meat-axe. I unlocked the kitchen door an' went in, with the axe in one hand an' the meat in the other. The dog might take his choice. I knowed he must be pretty nigh famished, for there was nothin' that he could get at to eat. As soon as I went in, he came runnin' to me, but I could see he was shaky on his legs. He looked a-sort of wicked at me, an' then he grabbed the meat. He was all right then."

"Oh, my!" said Euphemia, "I am so glad to hear that. I was afraid you never got in. But we saw the dog—is he as savage yet?"

"Oh, no!" said Pomona, "nothin' like it."

"Look here, Pomona," said I, "I want to know about those taxes. When do they come into your story?"

"Pretty soon, sir," said she, and she went on:

"After that I knowed it wouldn't do to have them two dogs so that they'd have to be tied up if they see each other. Just as like as not I'd want them both at once, an' then they'd go to fightin', an' leave me to settle with some bloodthirsty lightnin'-rodder. So, as I knowed if they once had a fair fight an' found out which was master they'd be good friends afterward, I thought the best thing to do would be to let 'em fight it out, when there was nothin' else for 'em to do. So I fixed up things for the combat."

"Why, Pomona!" cried Euphemia, "I didn't think you were capable of such a cruel thing."

"It looks that way, ma'am, but really it ain't," replied the girl. "It seemed to me as if it would be a mercy to both of 'em to have the thing settled. So I cleared away a place in front of the woodshed, an' unchained Lord Edward, an' then I opened the kitchen door an' called the bull. Out he came, with his teeth a-showin', an' his bloodshot eyes, an' his crooked front legs. Like lightnin' from the mount'in blast, he made one bounce for the big dog, an' oh! what a fight there was! They rolled, they gnashed, they knocked over the wood-horse an' sent chips a-flyin' all ways at wonst. I thought Lord Edward would whip in a minute or two, but he didn't, for the bull stuck to him like a burr; they was havin' it, ground an' lofty, when I hears some one run up behind me, an' turnin' quick, there was the 'Piscopalian minister. 'My! my! my!' he hollers. 'What a awful spectacle! Ain't there no way of stoppin' it?' 'No, sir,' says I; an' I told him how I didn't want to stop it, an' the reason why. Then says he, 'Where's your master?' An' I told him how you was away. 'Isn't there any man at all about?' says he. 'No,' says I. 'Then,' says he, 'if there's nobody else to stop

it, I must do it myself.' An' he took off his coat.
'No,' says I, 'you keep back, sir. If there's anybody
to plunge into that erena, the blood be mine;' an' I
put my hand, without thinkin', ag'in' his black shirt-
bosom, to hold him back; but he didn't notice, bein'
so excited. 'Now,' says I, 'jist wait one minute, and
you'll see that bull's tail go between his legs. He's
weakenin'.' An' sure enough, Lord Edward got a
good grab at him, an' was a-shakin' the very life out
of him, when I run up an' took Lord Edward by the
collar. 'Drop it!' says I, an' he dropped it, for he
knowed he'd whipped, an' he was pretty tired hisself.
Then the bull-dog he trotted off with his tail a-hangin'
down. 'Now, then,' says I, 'them dogs will be bosom
friends forever after this.' 'Ah, me!' says he, 'I'm
sorry indeed that your employer, for who I've always
had a great respect, should allow you to get into such
habits.' That made me feel real bad, an' I told him,
mighty quick, that you was the last man in the world
to let me do anything like that, an' that, if you'd 'a'
been here, you'd 'a' separated them dogs, if they'd
a-chawed your arms off; that you was very particular
about such things; an' that it would be a pity if he
was to think you was a dog-fightin' gentleman, when
I'd often heard you say that, now you was fixed an'
settled, the one thing you would like most would be
to be made a vestryman."

I sat up straight in my chair.

"Pomona!" I exclaimed, "you didn't tell him
that?"

"That's what I said, sir, for I wanted him to know
what you really was; an' he says, 'Well, well, I never
knew that. It might be a very good thing. I'll speak

to some of the members about it. There's two vacan-
cies now in our vestry."

I was crushed; but Euphemia tried to put the
matter into the brightest light.

"Perhaps it may all turn out for the best," she said,
"and you may be elected, and that would be splendid.
But it would be an awfully funny thing for a dog-fight
to make you a vestryman."

I could not talk on this subject. "Go on, Pomona,"
I said, trying to feel resigned to my shame, "and tell
us about that poster on the fence."

"I'll be to that almost right away," she said. "It
was two or three days after the dog-fight that I was
down at the barn, an' happenin' to look over to Old
John's, I saw that tree-man there. He was a-showin'
his book to John, an' him an' his wife an' all the
young ones was a-standin' there, drinkin' down them
big peaches an' pears as if they was all real. I
knowed he'd come here ag'in, for them fellers never
gives you up; an' I didn't know how to keep him
away, for I didn't want to let the dogs loose on a man
what, after all, didn't want to do no more harm than
to talk the life out of you. So I just happened to
notice, as I came to the house, how kind of desolate
everything looked, an' I thought perhaps I might
make it look worse, an' he wouldn't care to deal here.
So I thought of puttin' up a poster like that, for nobody whose place was a-goin' to be sold for taxes would
be likely to want trees. So I run in the house, an'
wrote it quick, an' put it up. An' sure enough, the
man he come along soon, an' when he looked at that
paper, an' tried the gate, an' looked over the fence
an' saw the house all shut up an' not a livin' soul

about,—for I had both the dogs in the house with me, —he shook his head an' walked off, as much as to say, 'If that man had fixed his place up proper with my trees, he wouldn't 'a' come to this!' An' then, as I found the poster worked so good, I thought it might keep other people from comin' a-botherin' around, an' so I left it up; but I was a-goin' to be sure an' take it down before you came."

As it was now pretty late in the afternoon, I proposed that Pomona should postpone the rest of her narrative until evening. She said that there was nothing else to tell that was very particular, and I did not feel as if I could stand anything more just now, even if it were very particular.

When we were alone, I said to Euphemia:

"If we ever have to go away from this place again—"

"But we won't go away," she interrupted, looking up to me with as bright a face as she ever had, "at least, not for a long, long, long time to come. And I'm so glad you're to be a vestryman."

CHAPTER XIV

POMONA TAKES A BRIDAL TRIP

OUR life at Rudder Grange seemed to be in no way materially changed by my becoming a vestryman. The cow gave about as much milk as before, and the hens laid the usual number of eggs. Euphemia went to church with a little more of an air, perhaps; but as the wardens were never absent, and I was never, therefore, called upon to assist in taking up the collection, her sense of my position was not inordinately manifested.

For a year or two, indeed, there was no radical change in anything about Rudder Grange, except in Pomona. In her there was a change. She grew up.

She performed this feat quite suddenly. She was a young girl when she first came to us, and we had never considered her as anything else, when one evening a young man came to see her. Then we knew she had grown up.

We made no objections to her visitors,—she had several, from time to time,—"For," said Euphemia, "suppose my parents had objected to your visits." I could not consider the mere possibility of anything like this, and we gave Pomona all the ordinary opportunities for entertaining her visitors. To tell the truth, I think we gave her more than the ordinary opportunities. I know that Euphemia would wait on herself to almost any extent, rather than call upon Pomona when the latter was entertaining an evening visitor in the kitchen or on the back porch.

"Suppose my mother," she once remarked, in answer to a mild remonstrance from me in regard to a circumstance of this nature,—"suppose my mother had rushed into our presence when we were plighting our vows, and had told me to go down into the cellar and crack ice!"

It was of no use to talk to Euphemia on such subjects; she always had an answer ready.

"You don't want Pomona to go off and be married, do you?" I asked, one day, as she was putting up some new muslin curtains in the kitchen. "You seem to be helping her to do this all you can, and yet I don't know where on earth you will get another girl who will suit you so well."

"I don't know, either," replied Euphemia, with a tack in her mouth, "and I'm sure I don't want her to go. But neither do I want winter to come, or to have to wear spectacles; but I suppose both of these things will happen, whether I like it or not."

For some time after this Pomona had very little company, and we began to think that there was no danger of any present matrimonial engagement on her part,—a thought which was very gratifying to us, although we did not wish in any way to interfere with her prospects,—when, one afternoon, she quietly went to the village and was married.

Her husband was a tall young fellow, the son of a farmer in the county, who had occasionally been to see her, but whom she must have frequently met on her "afternoons out."

When Pomona came home and told us this news we were certainly well surprised.

"What on earth are we to do for a girl?" cried Euphemia.

"You're to have me till you can get another one," said Pomona, quietly. "I hope you don't think I'd go 'way an' leave you without anybody."

"But a wife ought to go to her husband," said Euphemia, "especially so recent a bride. Why didn't you let me know all about it? I would have helped to fit you out. We would have given you the nicest kind of a little wedding."

"I know that," said Pomona, "you're jus' good enough. But I didn't want to put you to all that trouble—right in preserving-time, too. An' he wanted it quiet, for he's awful backward about shows. An' as I'm to go to live with his folks,—at least, in a little house on the farm,—I might as well stay here as any-where, even if I didn't want to, for I can't go there till after frost."

"Why not?" I asked.

"The chills and fever," said she. "They have it awful down in that valley. Why, he had a chill while we was bein' married, right at the bridal altar."

"You don't say so!" exclaimed Euphemia. "How dreadful!"

"Yes, indeed," said Pomona. "He must 'a' forgot it was his chill-day, an' he didn't take his quinine, an' so it come on him jus' as he was a-promisin' to love an' pertect. But he stuck it out at the minister's house, an' walked home by hisself to finish his chill."

"And you didn't go with him?" cried Euphemia, indignantly.

"He said no. It was better thus. He felt it weren't the right thing to mingle the agur with his marriage vows. He promised to take sixteen grains to-morrow, an' so I came away. He'll be all right in a month or so, an' then we'll go an' keep house. You see, it ain't likely I could help him any by goin' there an' gettin' it myself."

"Pomona," said Euphemia, "this is dreadful. You ought to go and take a bridal tour and get him rid of those fearful chills."

"I never thought of that," said Pomona, her face lighting up wonderfully.

Now that Euphemia had fallen upon this happy idea, she never dropped it until she had made all the necessary plans and had put them into execution. In the course of a week she had engaged another servant, and had started Pomona and her husband off on a bridal tour, stipulating nothing but that they should take plenty of quinine in their trunk.

It was about three weeks after this, and Euphemia and I were sitting on our front steps,—I had come home early, and we had been potting some of the tenderest plants,—when Pomona walked in at the gate. She looked well, and had on a very bright new dress. Euphemia noticed this the moment she came in. We welcomed her warmly, for we felt a great interest in this girl, who had grown up in our family and under our care.

"Have you had your bridal trip?" asked Euphemia.

"Oh, yes!" said Pomona. "It's all over an' done with, an' we're settled in our house."

"Well, sit right down here on the steps and tell us all about it," said Euphemia, in a glow of delightful expectancy; and Pomona, nothing loath, sat down and told her tale.

"You see," said she, untying her bonnet strings to give an easier movement to her chin, "we didn't say where we was goin' when we started out, for the truth was, we didn't know. We couldn't afford to take no big trip, an' yet we wanted to do the thing up jus' as right as we could, seein' as you had set your heart on it, an' as we had, too, for that matter. Niagery Fall was what I wanted, but he said that it cost so much to see the sights there that he hadn't money to spare to take us there an' pay for all the sight-seein', too. We might go, he said, without seein' the sights, or, if there was any way of seein' the sights without goin', that might do; but he couldn't do both. So we give that up, an' after thinkin' a good deal, we agreed to go to some other falls, which might come cheaper, an' maybe be jus' as good to begin on. So we thought of Passaic Falls, up to Paterson; an' we went there, an' took a room at a little hotel, an' walked over to the falls. But they wasn't no good, after all, for there wasn't no water runnin' over 'em. There was rocks, an' precipicers, an' direful depths, an' everything for a good falls, except water, an' that was all bein' used at the mills. 'Well, Miguel,' says I, 'this is about as nice a place for a falls as ever I see, but—'"

"Miguel!" cried Euphemia. "Is that your husband's name?"

"Well, no," said Pomona, "it isn't. His given name is Jonas; but I hated to call him Jonas, an' on a bridal trip, too. He might jus' as well have had a more romantic-er name, if his parents had 'a' thought of it. So I determined I'd give him a better one while we was on our journey, anyhow, an' I changed his name to Miguel, which was the name of a Spanish count. He wanted me to call him Jiguel, because, he said, that would have a kind of a floatin' smell of his old name; but I didn't never do it. Well, neither of us didn't care to stay about no dry falls, so we went back to the hotel an' got our supper, an' begun to wonder what we should do next day. He said we'd better put it off an' dream about it, an' make up our minds nex' mornin', which I agreed to; an' that evenin', as we was sittin' in our room, I asked Miguel to tell me the story of his life. He said, at first, it hadn't none; but when I seemed a-kinder put out at this, he told me I mustn't mind, an' he would reveal the whole. So he told me this story :

"'My grandfather,' said he, 'was a rich and powerful Portugee, a-livin' on the island of Jamaica. He had heaps o' slaves, an' owned a black brigantine, that he sailed in on secret voyages, an' when he come back the decks an' the gunnels was often bloody, but nobody knew why or wherefore. He was a big man with black hair an' very violent. He could never have kept no help if he hadn't owned 'em, but he was so rich that people respected him, in spite of all his crimes. My grandmother was a native o' the Isle o' Wight. She was a frail an' tender woman, with yeller hair an' deep blue eyes, an' gentle, an' soft, an' good to the poor. She used to take baskits of vittles aroun' to sick folks, an' set down on the side o' their beds an' read "The Shepherd o' Salisbury Plains" to 'em. She hardly ever speaked above her breath, an' always wore white gowns with a silk kerchief a-folded placidly aroun' her neck.' 'Them was awful different kind o' people,' I says to him. 'I wonder how they ever come to be married.' 'They never was married,' says he. 'Never married!' I hollers, a-jumpin' up from my chair, 'an' you sit there carmly an' look me in the eye.' 'Yes,' says he, 'they was never married. They never met; one was my mother's father, an' the other one my father's mother. 'Twas well they did not wed.' 'I should think so,' said I; 'an' now, what's the good of tellin' me a thing like that?'

"'It's about as near the mark as most of the stories of people's lives, I reckon,' says he; 'an' besides, I'd only jus' begun it.'

"'Well, I don't want no more,' says I; an' I jus' tell this story of his to show what kind of stories he told about that time. He said they was pleasant fictions, but I told him that if he didn't look out he'd hear 'em called by a good deal of a worse kind of a name than that. The nex' mornin' he asked me what was my dream, an' I told him I didn't have exactly no dream about it, but my idea was to have somethin' real romantic for the rest of our bridal days.

"'Well,' says he, 'what would you like? I had a dream, but it wasn't noways romantic, an' I'll jus' fall in with whatever you'd like best.'

"'All right,' says I; 'an' the most romantic-est thing that I can think of is for us to make believe for the rest of this trip. We can make believe we're anything we please, an' if we think so in real earnest it will be pretty much the same thing as if we really was. We ain't likely to have no chance ag'in of being jus' what we've a mind to, an' so let's try it now.'

"'What would you have a mind to be?' says he.

"'Well,' says I, 'let's be an earl an' a earl-ess.'

"'Earl-ess?' says he. 'There's no such a person.'

"'Why, yes, there is, of course,' I says to him. 'What's a she-earl, if she isn't a earl-ess?'

"'Well, I don't know,' says he, 'never havin' lived with any of 'em. But we'll let it go at that. An' how do you want to work the thing out?'

"'This way,' says I. 'You, Miguel—'

"'Jiguel,' says he.

"'The earl,' says I, not mindin' his interruption, 'an' me, your noble earl-ess, will go to some good place or other,—it don't matter much jus' where,—an' whatever house we live in we'll call our castle, an' we'll consider it's got drawbridges an' portcullises an' moats an' secrit dungeons, an' we'll remember our noble ancestors, an' behave accordin'. An' the people we meet we can make into counts an' dukes an' princes, without their knowin' anything about it; an' we can think our clothes is silk an' satin an' velvet, all covered with dimuns an' precious stones, jus' as well as not.'

"'Jus' as well,' says he.

"'An' then,' I went on, 'we can go an' have chi-*val*-rous adventures,—or make believe we're havin' 'em, —an' build up a atmosphere of romanticness aroun' us that'll carry us back—'

"'To ole Virginny,' says he.

"'No,' says I, 'for thousands of years, or at least enough back for the times of tournaments and chi-*val*-ry.'

"'An' so your idea is that we make believe all these things, an' don't pay for none of 'em, is it?' says he.

171

"'Yes,' says I; 'an' you, Miguel—'

"'Jiguel,' says he.

"'Can ask me, if you don't know, what chi-*val*-ric or romantic thing you ought to do or to say so as to feel yourself truly an' reely a earl, for I've read a lot about these people, an' know jus' what ought to be did.'

"Well, he set himself down an' thought awhile, an' then he says : 'All right ; we'll do that ; an' we'll begin to-morrow mornin', for I've got a little business to do in the city which wouldn't be exactly the right thing for me to stoop to after I'm a earl, so I'll go in an' do it while I'm a common person, an' come back this afternoon ; an' you can walk about an' look at the dry falls, an' amuse yourself gen'rally, till I come back.'

"'All right,' says I, an' off he goes.

"He come back afore dark, an' the nex' mornin' we got ready to start off.

"'Have you any particular place to go?' says he.

"'No,' says I ; 'one place is as likely to be as good as another for our style o' thing. If it don't suit, we can imagine it does.'

"'That'll do,' says he, an' we had our trunk sent to the station, an' walked ourselves. When we got there, he says to me :

"'Which number will you have, five or seven?'

"'Either one will suit me, Earl Miguel,' says I.

"'Jiguel,' says he, 'an' we'll make it seven. An' now I'll go an' look at the time-table, an' we'll buy tickets for the seventh station from here. The seventh station,' says he, comin' back, 'is Pokus. We'll go to Pokus.'

"So when the train come we got in, an' got out at Pokus. It was a pretty sort of a place, out in the

RUDDER GRANGE

country, with the houses scattered a long ways apart, like stingy chicken-feed.

"'Let's walk down this road,' says he, 'till we come to a good house for a castle, an' then we can ask 'em to take us to board, an' if they won't do it we'll go to the next, an' so on.'

"'All right,' says I, glad enough to see how pat he entered into the thing.

"We walked a good ways, an' passed some little houses that neither of us thought would do without more imaginin' than would pay, till we came to a pretty big house near the river, which struck our fancy in a minute. It was a stone house, an' it had trees aroun' it; there was a garden with a wall, an' things seemed to suit first-rate, so we made up our minds right off that we'd try this place.

"'You wait here under this tree,' says he, 'an' I'll go an' ask 'em if they'll take us to board for a while.'

"So I waits, an' he goes up to the gate, an' pretty soon he comes out an' says, 'All right, they'll take us, an' they'll send a man with a wheelbarrer to the station for our trunk.' So in we goes. The man was a country-like lookin' man, an' his wife was a very pleasant woman. The house wasn't furnished very fine, but we didn't care for that, an' they gave us a big room that had rafters instid of a ceilin', an' a big fireplace, an' that, I said, was jus' exac'ly what we wanted. The room was almos' like a donjon itself, which he said he reckoned had once been a kitchin; but I told him that a earl hadn't nothin' to do with kitchins, an' that this was a tapestry chamber, an' I'd tell him all about the strange figgers on the embroidered hangin's when the shadders begun to fall.

173

"It rained a little that afternoon, an' we stayed in our room, an' hung our clothes an' things about on nails an' hooks, an' made believe they was armor an' ancient trophies an' portraits of a long line of ancesters. I did most of the make believin'; but he agreed to ev'rything. The man who kep' the house's wife brought us our supper about dark, because she said she thought we might like to have it together cosey, an' so we did, an' was glad enough of it; an' after supper we sat before the fireplace, where we made believe the flames was a-roarin' an' cracklin' an' a-lightin' up the bright places on the armor a-hangin' aroun', while the storm—which we made believe—was a-ragin' an' whirlin' outside. I told him a long story about a lord an' a lady, which was two or three stories I had read run together, an' we had a splendid time. It all seemed real real to me."

CHAPTER XV

"THE nex' mornin' was fine an' nice," continued Pomona, "an' after our breakfast had been brought to us, we went out in the grounds to take a walk. There was lots of trees back of the house, with walks among 'em, an' altogether it was so ole-timey an' castleish that I was as happy as a lark.

"'Come along, Earl Miguel,' I says, 'let us tread a measure 'neath these mantlin' trees.'

"'All right,' says he. 'Your Jiguel attends you. An' what might our noble second name be? What is we earl an' earl-ess of?'

"'Oh, anything,' says I. 'Let's take any name at random.'

"'All right,' says he. 'Let it be random. Earl an' Earl-ess Random. Come along.'

"So we walks about, I feelin' mighty noble an' springy, an' afore long we sees another couple a-walkin' about under the trees.

"'Who's them?' says I.

"'Don't know,' says he, 'but I expect they're some

175

o' the other boarders. The man said he had other
boarders when I spoke to him about takin' us.'

"'Let's make believe they're a count an' countess,'
says I. 'Count an' Countess of—'

"'Milwaukee,' says he.

"I didn't think much of this for a noble name, but
still it would do well enough, an' so we called 'em the
Count an' Countess of Milwaukee, an' we kep' on a-
meanderin'. Pretty soon he gets tired an' says he was
a-goin' back to the house to have a smoke, because he
thought it was time to have a little fun which weren't
all imaginations ; an' I says to him to go along, but it
would be the hardest thing in this world for me to
imagine any fun in smokin'. He laughed an' went
back, while I walked on, a-makin' believe a page
in blue puffed breeches was a-holdin' up my train,
which was of light-green velvet trimmed with silver
lace. Pretty soon, turnin' a little corner, I meets the
Count and Countess of Milwaukee. She was a small
lady, dressed in black, an' he was a big fat man about
fifty years old, with a grayish beard. They both wore
little straw hats, exac'ly alike, an' had on green carpet-slippers.

"They stops when they sees me, an' the lady she
bows an' says 'Good mornin' ;' an' then she smiles very
pleasant, an' asks if I was a-livin' here, an' when I
said I was, she says she was too, for the present, an'
what was my name. I had half a mind to say the
Earl-ess Random, but she was so pleasant and sociable
that I didn't like to seem to be makin' fun, an' so I
said I was Mrs. de Henderson.

"'An' I,' says she, 'am Mrs. General Andrew Jackson, widow of the ex-President of the United States.

I am staying here on business connected with the United States Bank. This is my brother,' says she, pointin' to the big man.

"'How d'ye do?' says he, a-puttin' his hands together, turnin' his toes out, an' makin' a funny little bow. 'I am General Tom Thumb,' he says in a deep, gruff voice, 'an' I've been before all the crown-ed heads of Europe, Asia, Africa, America, an' Australia, —all *a*'s but one,—an' I'm waitin' here for a team of four little milk-white oxen, no bigger than tall cats, which is to be hitched to a little hay-wagon, which I am to ride in, with a little pitchfork an' real farmer's clothes, only small. This will come to-morrow, when I will pay for it an' ride away to exhibit. It may be here now, an' I will go an' see. Good-by.'

"'Good-by, likewise,' says the lady. 'I hope you'll have all you're thinkin' you're havin', an' more too, but less if you'd like it. Farewell.' An' away they goes.

"Well, you may be sure I stood there amazed enough, an' mad, too, when I heard her talk about my bein' all I was a-thinkin' I was. I was sure my husband—scarce two weeks old a husband—had told all. It was too bad. I wished I had jus' said I was the Earl-ess of Random an' brassed it out.

"I rushed back, an' foun' him smokin' a pipe on a back porch. I charged him with his perfidy, but he vowed so earnest that he had not told these people of our fancies, or ever had spoke to 'em, that I had to believe him.

"'I expec',' says he, 'that they're jus' makin' believe —as we are. There ain't no patent on make-believes.'

"This didn't satisfy me, an' as he seemed to be so

careless about it, I walked away an' left him to his pipe. I determined to go take a walk along some of the country roads an' think this thing over for myself. I went aroun' to the front gate, where the woman of the house was a-standin' talkin' to somebody, an' I jus' bowed to her, for I didn't feel like sayin' anything, an' walked past her.

"'Hello!' said she, jumpin' in front of me an' shuttin' the gate. 'You can't go out here. If you want to walk you can walk about in the grounds. There's lots of shady paths.'

"'Can't go out!' says I. 'Can't go out! What do you mean by that?'

"'I mean jus' what I say,' said she, an' she locked the gate.

"I was so mad that I could have pushed her over an' broke the gate; but I thought that if there was anything of that kind to do I had a husband whose business it was to attend to it, an' so I runs aroun' to him to tell him. He had gone in, but I met Mrs. Jackson an' her brother.

"'What's the matter?' said she, seein' what a hurry I was in.

"'That woman at the gate,' I said, almost chokin' as I spoke, 'won't let me out.'

"'She won't?' said Mrs. Jackson. 'Well, that's a way she has. Four times the Bank of the United States has closed its doors before I was able to get there, on account of that woman's obstinacy about the gate. Indeed, I have not been to the bank at all yet, for of course it is of no use to go after banking hours.'

"'An' I believe, too,' said her brother, in his heavy

178

voice, 'that she has kept out my team of little oxen. Otherwise it would be here now.'

"I couldn't stand any more of this, an' ran into our room, where my husband was. When I told him what had happened, he was real sorry.

"'I didn't know you thought of going out,' he said, 'or I would have told you all about it. An' now, sit down an' quiet yourself, an' I'll tell you jus' how things is.' So down we sits, an' says he, jus' as carm as a summer cloud, 'My dear, this is a lunertic asylum. Now, don't jump,' he says; 'I didn't bring you here because I thought you was crazy, but because I wanted you to see what kind of people they was who imagined themselves earls and earl-esses, an' all that sort o' thing, an' to have an idea how the thing worked after you'd been doing it a good while an' had got used to it. I thought it would be a good thing, while I was Earl Jiguel and you was a noble earl-ess, to come to a place where people acted that way. I knowed you had read lots o' books about knights and princes an' bloody towers, an' that you knowed all about them things, but I didn't suppose you did know how them same things looked in these days, an' a lunertic asylum was the only place where you could see 'em. So I went to a doctor I knowed,' he says, 'an' got a certificate from him to this private institution, where we could stay for a while an' get posted on romantics.'

"'Then,' says I, 'the upshot was that you wanted to teach a lesson.'

"'Jus' that,' says he.

"'All right,' says I, 'it's teached. An' now let's get out of this as quick as we kin.'

"'That'll suit me,' he says, 'an' we'll leave by the

noon train. I'll go an' see about the trunk bein' sent down.'

"So off he went to see the man who kept the house, while I falls to packin' up the trunk as fast as I could."

"Weren't you dreadfully angry at him?" asked Euphemia, who, having a romantic streak in her own composition, did not sympathize altogether with this heroic remedy for Pomona's disease.

"No, ma'am," said Pomona, "not long. When I thought of Mrs. General Jackson an' Tom Thumb, I couldn't help thinkin' that I must have looked pretty much the same to my husband, who, I knowed now, had only been makin' believe to make believe. An' besides, I couldn't be angry very long, for laughin', for when he come back in a minute, as mad as a March hare, an' said they wouldn't let me out, nor him nuther, I fell to laughin' ready to crack my sides.

"'They say,' said he, as soon as he could speak straight, 'that we can't go out without another certificate from the doctor. I told 'em I'd go myself an' see him about it; but they said no, I couldn't, for if they did that way everybody who ever was sent here would be goin' out the next day to see about leavin'. I didn't want to make no fuss, so I told them I'd write a letter to the doctor an' tell him to send an order that would soon show them whether we could go out or not. They said that would be the best thing to do, an' so I'm goin' to write it this minute'—which he did.

"'How long will we have to wait?' says I, when the letter was done.

"'Well,' says he, 'the doctor can't get this before to-morrow mornin', an' even if he answers right away, we won't get our order to go out until the next day. So we'll jus' have to grin an' bear it for a day an' a half.'

"'This is a lively old bridal trip,' said I—'dry falls an' a lunertic asylum.'

"'We'll try to make the rest of it better,' said he.

"But the next day wasn't no better. We stayed in our room all day, for we didn't care to meet Mrs. Jackson an' her crazy brother, an' I'm sure we didn't want to see the mean creatures who kept the house. We knew well enough that they only wanted us to stay so that they could get more board-money out of us."

"I should have broken out," cried Euphemia. "I would never have stayed an hour in that place after I found out what it was, especially on a bridal trip."

"If we'd done that," said Pomona, "they'd have got men after us, an' then everybody would have thought we was real crazy. We made up our minds to wait for the doctor's letter; but it wasn't much fun. An' I didn't tell no romantic stories to fill up the time. We sat down an' behaved like the commonest kind o' people. You never saw anybody sicker of romantics than I was when I thought of them two loons that called themselves Mrs. Andrew Jackson and General Tom Thumb. I dropped Miguel altogether, an' he dropped Jiguel, which was a relief to me, an' I took strong to Jonas, even callin' him Jone, which I consider a good deal uglier an' commoner even than Jonas. He didn't like this much, but said that if it would help me out of the Miguel, he didn't care.

"Well, on the mornin' of the next day I went into the little front room that they called the office, to see if there was a letter for us yet, an' there wasn't no-

181

body there to ask. But I saw a pile of letters under a weight on the table, an' I jus' looked at these to see if one of 'em was for us, an' if there wasn't the very letter Jone had written to the doctor! They'd never sent it! I rushed back to Jone an' told him, an' he jus' set an' looked at me without sayin' a word. I didn't wonder he couldn't speak.

"'I'll go an' let them people know what I think of 'em,' says I.

"'Don't do that,' said Jone, catchin' me by the sleeve. 'It won't do no good. Leave the letter there, an' don't say nothin' about it. We'll stay here till afternoon quite quiet, an' then we'll go away. That garden wall isn't high.'

"'An' how about the trunk?' says I.

"'Oh, we'll take a few things in our pockets, an' lock up the trunk, an' ask the doctor to send for it when we get to the city.'

"'All right,' says I. An' we went to work to get ready to leave.

"About five o'clock in the afternoon, when it was a nice time to take a walk under the trees, we meandered quietly down to a corner of the back wall where Jone thought it would be rather convenient to get over. He hunted up a short piece of board, which he leaned up ag'in' the wall, an' then he put his foot on the top of that an' got hold of the top of the wall an' climbed up, as easy as nothin'. Then he reached down to help me step onto the board. But jus' as he was a-goin' to take me by the hand, 'Hello,' says he, 'look-a-there!' An' I turned round an' looked, an' if there wasn't Mrs. Andrew Jackson an' General Tom Thumb a-walkin' down the path.

"Hello! Look a-there!"

"'What shall we do?' says I.

"'Come along,' says he. 'We ain't a-goin' to stop for them. Get up, all the same.'

"I tried to get up as he said, but it wasn't so easy for me on account of my not bein' such a high-stepper as Jone, an' I was a good while a-gettin' a good footin' on the board.

"Mrs. Jackson an' the General they came right up to us, an' set down on a bench which was fastened between two trees near the wall. An' there they set, a-lookin' steady at us with their four little eyes, like four empty thimbles.

"'You appear to be goin' away,' says Mrs. Jackson.

"'Yes,' says Jone from the top of the wall. 'We're a-goin' to take a slight stroll outside, this salu-brious evenin'.'

"'Do you think,' says she, 'that the United States Bank would be open this time of day?'

"'Oh, no,' says Jone, 'the banks all close at three o'clock. It's a good deal after that now.'

"'But if I told the officers who I was, wouldn't that make a difference?' says she. 'Wouldn't they go down an' open the bank?'

"'Not much,' says Jone, givin' a pull which brought me right up to the top o' the wall an' almost clean down the other side with one jerk. 'I never knowed no officers that would do that. But,' says he, a-kind o' shuttin' his eyes so that she shouldn't see he was lyin', 'we'll talk about that when we come back.'

"'If you see that team of little oxen,' says the big man, 'send 'em round to the front gate.'

"'All right,' says Jone; an' he let me down the outside of the wall as if I had been a bag o' horse-feed.

"'But if the bank isn't open you can't pay for it when it does come,' we heard the old lady a-sayin', as we hurried off.

"We didn't lose no time a-goin' down to that station, an' it's lucky we didn't, for a train for the city was comin' jus' as we got there, an' we jumped aboard without havin' no time to buy tickets. There wasn't many people in our car, an' we got a seat together.

"'Now, then,' says Jone, as the cars went a-buzzin' along, 'I feel as if I was really on a bridal trip, which I mus' say I didn't at that there asylum.'

"An' then I said, 'I should think not,' an' we both bust out a-laughin', as well we might, feelin' sich a change of surroundin's.

"'Do you think,' says somebody behind us, when we'd got through laughin', 'that if I was to send a boy up to the cashier he would either come down or send me the key of the bank?'

"We both turned aroun' as quick as lightnin', an' if there wasn't them two lunertics in the seat behind us!

"It nearly took our breaths away to see them settin' there, staring at us with their thimble eyes, an' a-wearin' their little straw hats, both alike.

"'How on the livin' earth did you two get here?' says I, as soon as I could speak.

"'Oh, we come by the same way you come—by the tem-per-ary stairs,' says Mrs. Jackson. 'We thought if it was too late to draw any money to-night, it might be well to be on hand bright an' early in the mornin'. An' so we follered you two as close as we could, because we knew you could take us right to the very

184

bank doors, an' we didn't know the way ourselves, not never havin' had no occasion to attend to nothin' of this kind before.'

"Jone an' I looked at each other, but we didn't speak for a minute.

"Then' says I, 'Here's a pretty kittle o' fish.'

"'I should kinder say so,' says Jone. 'We've got these here two lunertics on our hands, sure enough, for there ain't no train back to Pokus to-night, an' I wouldn't go back with 'em if there was. We must keep an eye on 'em till we can see the doctor to-morrow.'

"'I suppose we must,' says I, 'but this don't seem as much like a bridal trip as it did awhile ago.'

"'You're right there,' says Jone.

"When the conductor came along we had to pay the fare of them two lunertics, besides our own, for neither of 'em had a cent about 'em. When we got to town we went to a smallish hotel near the ferry, where Jone knowed the man who kep' it, who wouldn't bother about none of us havin' a scrap of baggage, knowin' he'd get his money all the same, out of either Jone or his father. The General an' his sister looked a-kind o' funny in their little straw hats an' green carpet-slippers, an' the clerk didn't know whether he hadn't forgot how to read writin' when the big man put down the names of General Tom Thumb and Mrs. ex-President Andrew Jackson, which he wasn't ex-President anyway, bein' dead ; but Jone he whispered they was travellin' under nommys dess plummys,—I told him to say that, an' he would fix it all right in the mornin'. An' then we got some sup-

RUDDER GRANGE

per,—which it took them two lunertics a long time to
eat, for they was all the time forgettin' what particular
kind o' business they was about,—an' then we was
showed to our rooms. They had two rooms right
across the hall from ours. We hadn't been inside our
room five minutes before Mrs. General Jackson come
a-knockin' at the door.

"'Look-a-here,' she says to me, 'there's a unforeseen
contingency in my room. An' it smells.'

"So I went right in, an' sure enough it did smell,
for she had turned on all the gases, besides the one
that was lighted.

"'What did you do that for?' says I, a-turnin' them
off as fast as I could.

"'I'd like to know what they're made for,' says she,
'if they isn't to be turned on.'

"When I told Jone about this he looked real serious,
an' jus' then a waiter came up-stairs an' went into the
big man's room. In a minute he come out an' says to
Jone an' me, a-grinnin':

"'We can't suit him no better in this house.'

"'What does he want?' asks Jone.

"'Why, he wants a smaller bed,' says the waiter.
'He says he can't sleep in a bed as big as that, an'
we haven't none smaller in this house, which he
couldn't get into if we had, in my opinion,' says he.

"'All right,' says Jone. 'Jus' you go down-stairs,
an' I'll fix him.' So the man goes off, still a-grinnin'.
'I tell you what it is,' says Jone, 'it won't do to let
them two lunertics have rooms to themselves. They'll
set this house afire or turn it upside down in the
middle of the night, if they has. There's nothin' to
be done but for you to sleep with the woman an' for

186

me to sleep with the man, to keep 'em from cuttin' up till mornin'.'

"So Jone he went into the room where General Tom Thumb was a-settin' with his hat on, a-lookin' doleful at the bed, an' says he :

"'What's the matter with the bed?'

"'Oh, it's too large entirely,' says the General. 'It wouldn't do for me to sleep in a bed like that. It would ruin my character as a genuine Thumb.'

"'Well,' says Jone, 'it's nearly two times too big for you, but if you an' me was both to sleep in it, it would be about right, wouldn't it?'

"'Oh yes,' says the General. An' he takes off his hat, an' Jone says good night to me an' shuts the door. Our room was better than Mrs. General Jackson's, so I takes her in there, an' the fust thing she does is to turn on all the gases.

"'Stop that!' I hollers. 'If you do that agin, I'll —I'll break the United States Bank to-morrow!'

"'How'll you do that?' says she.

"'I'll draw out all my capital,' says I.

"'I hope really you won't,' says she, 'till I've been there;' an' she leans out of the open winder to look into the street. But while she was a-lookin' out I see her left hand a-creepin' up to the gas by the winder, that wasn't lighted. I felt mad enough to take her by the feet an' pitch her out, as you an' the boarder," said Pomona, turning to me, "h'isted me out of the canal-boat winder."

This, by the way, was the first intimation we had had that Pomona knew how she came to fall out of that window.

"But I didn't do it," she continued, "for there

wasn't no soft water underneath for her to fall into. After we went to bed I kep' awake for a long time, bein' afraid she'd get up in the night an' turn on all the gases an' smother me alive. But I fell asleep at last, an' when I woke up, early in the mornin', the first thing I did was to feel for that lunertic. But she was gone !"

CHAPTER XVI

IN WHICH AN OLD FRIEND APPEARS AND THE BRIDAL TRIP TAKES A FRESH START

"Gone?" cried Euphemia, who, with myself, had been listening most intently to Pomona's story.

"Yes," continued Pomona, "she was gone. I give one jump out of bed an' felt the gases, but they was all right. But she was gone, an' her clothes was gone. I dressed, as pale as death, I do expect, an' hurried to Jone's room, an' he an' me an' the big man was all ready in no time to go an' look for her. General Tom Thumb didn't seem very anxious, but we made him hurry up an' come along with us. We couldn't afford to leave him nowheres. The clerk down-stairs—a different one from the chap who was there the night before—said that a middle-aged, elderly lady came down about an hour before an' asked him to tell her the way to the United States Bank, an' when he told her he didn't know of any such bank, she jus' stared at him, an' wanted to know what he was put there for. So he didn't have no more to say to her, an' she went out, an' he didn't take no notice which way she went. We had the same opinion about him that Mrs. Jackson had, but we didn't stop to tell him so. We hunted up an' down the streets

189

for an hour or more; we asked every policeman we met if he'd seen her; we went to a police station; we did everything we could think of, but no Mrs. Jackson turned up. Then we was so tired an' hungry we went into some place or other an' got our breakfast. When we started out ag'in, we kep' on up one street an' down another, askin' everybody who looked as if they had two grains of sense—which most of 'em didn't look as if they had mor'n one, an' that was in use to get 'em to where they was goin'. At last, a little ways down a small street, we seed a crowd, an' the minute we see it Jone an' me both said in our inside hearts, 'There she is!' An' sure enough, when we got there, who should we see, with a ring of street-loafers an' boys around her, but Mrs. Andrew Jackson, with her little straw hat an' her green carpet-slippers, a-dancin' some kind of a skippin' fandango, an' a-holdin' out her skirts with the tips of her fingers. I was jus' a-goin' to rush in an' grab her when a man walks quick into the ring an' touches her on the shoulder. The minute I seed him I knowed him. It was our old boarder!"

"It was?" exclaimed Euphemia.

"Yes, it was truly him; I didn't want him to see me there in such company, an' he most likely knowin' I was on my bridal trip, so I made a dive at my bonnet to see if I had a veil on, an' findin' one, I hauled it down.

"'Madam,' says the boarder, very respectful, to Mrs. Jackson, 'where do you live? Can't I take you home?' 'No, sir,' says she, 'at least, not now. If you have a carriage, you may come for me after a while. I am waiting for the Bank of the United States to

open, an' until which time I must support myself on
the light fantastic toe ; ' an' then she tuk up her skirts
an' begun to dance ag'in. But she didn't make mor'n
two skips before I rushed in, an' takin' her by the
arm, hauled her out o' the ring. An' then up comes
the big man, with his face as red as fire. 'Look here !'
says he to her, as if he was ready to eat her up. 'Did
you draw every cent of that money ?' 'Not yet, not
yet,' says she. 'You did, you purse-proud cantalope,'
says he. 'You know very well you did. An' now I'd
like to know where my ox-money is to come from.'
But Jone an' me didn't intend to wait for no sich talk
as this, so he tuk the man by the arm, an' I tuk the
old woman, an' we jus' walked 'em off. The boarder
he told the loafers to get out an' go home, an' none
of 'em follered us, for they knowed if they did he'd 'a'
batted 'em over the head. But he comes up alongside
o' me as I was a-walkin' behind with Mrs. Jackson,
an' says he : 'How d'ye do, Pomona ?' I must say I
felt as if I could slip in between two flagstones ; but as
I couldn't get away, I said I was pretty well. 'I
heared you was on your bridal trip,' says he, ag'in ; 'is
this it ?' It was jus' like him to know that, an' as
there was no help for it, I said it was. 'Is that your
husband ?' says he, pointin' to Jone. 'Yes,' says I.
'It was very good in him to come along', says he. 'Is
these two your groomsman and bridesmaid ?' 'No,
sir,' says I. 'They're crazy.' 'No wonder,' says he.
'It's enough to drive 'em so, to see you two ; ' an' then
he went ahead an' shook hands with Jone, an' told him
he'd knowed me a long time ; but he didn't say nothin'
about havin' h'isted me out of a winder, for which
I was obliged to him. Then he come back to me,

an' says he : 'Good mornin' ; I must go to the office. I hope you'll have a good time for the rest of your trip. If you happen to run short o' lunertics, jus' let me know, an' I'll furnish you with another pair.' 'All right,' says I, 'but you mustn't bring your little girl along.'

"He kinder laughed at this as we walked away, an' then he turned around an' come back, an' says he, 'Have you been to any the-ay-ters, or anything, since you've been in town?' 'No,' says I, 'not one.' 'Well,' says he, 'you ought to go. Which do you like best, the the-ay-ter, the cir-cus, or wild beasts?' I did really like the the-ay-ter best, havin' thought of bein' a play-actor, as you know, but I considered I'd better let that kind o' thing slide jus' now, as bein' a little too romantic, right after the 'sylum, so I says, 'I've been once to a circus, an' once to a wild-beast garden, an' I like 'em both. I hardly know which I like best —the roarin' beasts, a-prancin' about in their cages, with the smell of blood an' hay, an' the towerin' ele- phants ; or the horses, an' the music, an' the gauzy figgers at the circus, an' the splendid knights in armor an' flashin' pennants, all on fiery steeds, a-plungin' ag'in' the sides of the ring, with their flags a-flyin' in the grand entry,' says I, real excited with what I re- membered about these shows.

"'Well,' says he, 'I don't wonder at your feelin's. An' now, here's two tickets for to-night, which you an' your husband can have, if you like, for I can't go. They're to a meetin' of the Hudson County Enter-mo- logical Society, over to Hoboken, at eight o'clock.'

"'Over to Hoboken !' says I. 'That's a long way.'

"'Oh, no, it isn't,' says he. 'An' it won't cost you a

cent but the ferry. They couldn't have them shows in the city, for if the creatures was to get loose there's no knowin' what might happen. So take 'em, an' have as much fun as you can for the rest of your trip. Good-by !' An' off he went.

"Well, we kep' straight on to the doctor's, an' glad we was when we got there, an' mad he was when we lef' Mrs. Jackson an' the General on his hands, for we wouldn't have no more to do with 'em, an' he couldn't help undertakin' to see that they got back to the asylum. I thought at first he wouldn't lift a finger to get us our trunk ; but he cooled down after a bit, an' said he hoped we'd try some different kind of institution for the rest of our trip, which we said we thought we would.

"That afternoon we gawked around, a-lookin' at all the outside shows, for Jone said he'd have to be pretty careful of his money now, an' he was glad when I told him I had two free tickets in my pocket for a show in the evenin'.

"As we was a-walkin' down to the ferry, after supper, says he :

"'Suppose you let me have a look at them tickets.'

"So I hands 'em to him. He reads one of 'em, an' then he reads the other, which he needn't 'a' done, for they was both alike, an' then he turns to me an' says he :

"'What kind of a man is your boarder-as-was?'

"It wasn't the easiest thing in the world to say jus' what he was, but I give Jone the idea, in a general sort of way, that he was pretty lively.

"'So I should think,' says he. 'He's been tryin' a trick on us, an' sendin' us to the wrong place. It's rather late in the season for a show of the kind, but the place we ought to go to is a potato-field.'

"'What on earth are you talkin' about?' says I, dumfoundered.

"'Well,' says he, 'it's a trick he's been playin'. He thought a bridal trip like ours ought to have some sort of a outlandish wind-up, an' so he sent us to this place, which is a meetin' of chaps who are a-goin' to talk about insec's—principally potato-bugs, I expec'; an' anything stupider than that I s'pose your boarder-as-was couldn't think of, without havin' a good deal o' time to consider.'

"'It's jus' like him,' says I. 'Let's turn round an' go back,' which we did, prompt.

"We gave the tickets to a little boy who was sellin' papers, but I don't believe he went.

"'Now, then,' says Jone, after he'd been thinkin' awhile, 'there'll be no more foolin' on this trip. I've blocked out the whole of the rest of it, an' we'll wind up a sight better than that boarder-as-was has any idea of. To-morrow we'll go to father's, an' if the old gentleman has got any money on the crops, which I expec' he has by this time, I'll take up a part o' my share, an' we'll have a trip to Washington, an' see the President, an' Congress, an' the White House, an' the lamp always a-burnin' before the Supreme Court, an'—'

"'Don't say no more,' says I; 'it's splendid!'

"So, early the nex' day we goes off jus' as fast as trains would take us to his father's, an' we hadn't been there mor'n ten minutes before Jone found out he had been summoned on a jury.

"'When must you go?' says I, when he come, lookin' a-kind o' pale, to tell me this.

"'Right off,' says he. 'The court meets this mornin'. If I don't hurry up, I'll have some of 'em after me. But I wouldn't cry about it. I don't believe the case'll last mor'n a day.'

"The old man harnessed up an' took Jone to the court-house, an' I went too, for I might as well keep up the idea of a bridal trip as not. I went up into the gallery, an' Jone he was set among the other men in the jury-box.

"The case was about a man named Brown, who married the half-sister of a man named Adams, who afterward married Brown's mother, an' sold Brown a house he had got from Brown's grandfather, in trade for half a grist-mill, which the other half of was owned by Adams's half-sister's first husband, who left all his property to a soup society, in trust, till his son should come of age, which he never did, but left a will which give his half of the mill to Brown; the suit was between Brown an' Adams an' Brown again, an' Adams's half-sister, who was divorced from Brown, an' a man named Ramsey, who had put up a new overshot wheel to the grist-mill."

"Oh, my!" exclaimed Euphemia. "How could you remember all that?"

"I heard it so often, I couldn't help rememberin' it," replied Pomona, and she went on with her narrative:

"That case wasn't a easy one to understand, as you may see for yourselves, an' it didn't get finished that day. They argyed over it a full week. When there wasn't no more witnesses to carve up, one lawyer made a speech, an' he set that crooked case so straight that you could see through it from the overshot wheel clean back to Brown's grandfather. Then another feller made a speech, an' he set the whole thing up the other way. It was jus' as clear to look through, but it was another case altogether, no more like the other one than a apple-pie is like a mug o' cider. Then they both took it up, an' they swung it around between them, till it was all twisted an' knotted an' wound up an' tangled worse than a skein o' yarn in a nest o' kittens, an' then they give it to the jury.

"Well, when them jurymen went out, there wasn't none of 'em, as Jone told me afterward, as knew whether it was Brown or Adams as was dead, or whether the mill was to grind soup or to be run by soup-power. Of course they couldn't agree; three of 'em wanted to give a verdict for the boy that died, two of 'em was for Brown's grandfather, an' the rest was scattered, some goin' in for damages to the witnesses, who ought to get somethin' for havin' their char-*ac*-ters ruined. Jone he jus' held back, ready to jine the other eleven as soon as they'd agree. But they couldn't do it, an' they was locked up three days an' four nights. You'd better believe I got pretty wild about it, but I come to court every day an' waited an' waited, bringin' somethin' to eat in a baskit.

"One day, at dinner-time, I seed the judge a-standin' at the court-room door, a-wipin' his forrid with a handkerchief, an' I went up to him an' said, 'Do you think, sir, they'll get through this thing soon?'

"'I can't say, indeed,' said he. 'Are you interested in the case?'

"'I should think I was,' said I, an' then I told him about Jone's bein' a juryman, an' how we was on our bridal trip.

"'You've got my sympathy, madam,' says he, 'but it's a difficult case to decide, an' I don't wonder it takes a good while.'

"'Nor I, nuther,' says I. 'My opinion about these things is that if you'd jus' have them lawyers shut up in another room, an' make 'em do their talkin' to theirselves, the jury could keep their minds clear an' settle the cases in no time.'

"'There's some sense in that, madam,' says he, an' then he went into court ag'in.

"Jone never had no chance to jine in with the other fellers, for they couldn't agree, an' they were all discharged, at last. So the whole thing went for nothin'.

"When Jone come out, he looked like he'd been drawn through a pump-log, an' he says to me, tired-like :

"'Has there been a frost?'

"'Yes,' says I, 'two of 'em.'

"'All right, then,' says he. 'I've had enough of bridal trips, with their dry falls, their lunertic asylums, an' their jury-boxes. Let's go home an' settle down. We needn't be afraid, now that there's been a frost.'"

" Oh, why will you live in such a dreadful place?" cried Euphemia. "You ought to go to some place where you needn't be afraid of chills."

"That's jus' what I thought, ma'am," returned Pomona. "But Jone an' me got a disease-map of this country an' we looked all over it careful, an' wherever there wasn't chills there was somethin' that seemed a good deal wuss to us. An' says Jone, 'If I'm to have anything the matter with me, give me somethin' I'm

197

used to. It don't do for a man o' my time o' life to go changin' his diseases.'

"So home we went. An' there we is now. An' as this is the end of the bridal-trip story, I'll go an' take a look at the cow an' the chickens an' the horse, if you don't mind."

Which we did not, and we gladly went with her over the estate.

CHAPTER XVII

IN WHICH WE TAKE A VACATION AND LOOK FOR DAVID DUTTON

IT was about noon of a very fair July day, in the next summer, when Euphemia and myself arrived at the little town where we were to take a stage up into the mountains. We were off for a two weeks' vacation, and our minds were a good deal easier than when we went away before, and left Pomona at the helm. We had enlarged the boundaries of Rudder Grange, having purchased the house, with enough adjoining land to make quite a respectable farm. Of course I could not attend to the manifold duties on such a place, and my wife seldom had a happier thought than when she proposed that we should invite Pomona and her husband to come to live with us. Pomona was delighted, and Jonas was quite willing to run our farm. So arrangements were made, and the young couple were established in apartments in our back building, and went to work as if taking care of us and our possessions was the ultimate object of their lives. Jonas was such a steady fellow that we feared no trouble from tree-man or lightning-rodder during this absence.

Our destination was a country tavern on the stage-road, not far from the point where the road crosses the ridge of the mountain-range, and about sixteen miles from the town. We had heard of this tavern from a friend of ours who had spent a summer there. The surrounding country was lovely, and the house was kept by a farmer, who was a good soul and tried to make his guests happy. These were generally passing farmers and wagoners, or stage-passengers stopping for a meal; but occasionally a person from the cities, like our friend, came to spend a few weeks in the mountains.

So hither we came, for an out-of-the-world spot like this was just what we wanted. When I took our places at the stage office, I inquired for David Dutton, the farmer tavern-keeper before mentioned; but the agent did not know of him.

"However," said he, "the driver knows everybody on the road, and he'll set you down at the house."

So off we started, having paid for our tickets on the basis that we were to ride about sixteen miles. We had seats on top, and the trip, although slow,—for the road wound uphill steadily,—was a delightful one. Our way lay, for the greater part of the time, through the woods, but now and then we came to a farm, and a turn in the road often gave us lovely views of the foot-hills and the valleys behind us.

But the driver did not know where Dutton's tavern was. This we found out after we had started. Some persons might have thought it wiser to settle this matter before starting, but I am not at all sure that it would have been so. We were going to this tavern, and did not wish to go anywhere else. If people did not know where it was, it would be well for us to go

RUDDER GRANGE

to look for it. We knew the road that it was on, and the locality in which it was to be found.

Still, it was somewhat strange that a stage-driver, passing along the road every week-day,—one day one way, and the next the other way,—should not know a public house like Dutton's.

"If I remember rightly," I said, "the stage used to stop there for the passengers to take supper."

"Well, then, it ain't on this side o' the ridge," said the driver, "we stop for supper about a quarter of a mile on the other side, at Pete Lowry's. Perhaps Dutton used to keep that place. Was it called the 'Ridge House'?"

I did not remember the name of the house, but I knew very well that it was not on the other side of the ridge.

"Then," said the driver, "I'm sure I don't know where it is. But I've only been on the road about a year, an' your man may 'a' moved away afore I come. But there ain't no tavern this side the ridge arter ye leave Delhi, an' that's nowhere's nigh the ridge."

There were a couple of farmers sitting by the driver, who had listened with considerable interest to this conversation. Presently one of them turned around to me and said :

"Is it Dave Dutton ye're askin' about?"

"Yes," I replied, "that's his name."

"Well, I think he's dead," said he.

At this I began to feel uneasy, and I could see that my wife shared my trouble.

Then the other farmer spoke up.

"I don't believe he's dead, Hiram," said he to his companion. "I heared of him this spring. He's got a sheep-farm on the other side o' the mountain, an' he's a-livin' there. That's what I heared, at any rate. But he don't live on this road any more," he continued, turning to us. "He used to keep tavern on this road, an' the stages did used to stop fur supper —or else dinner, I don't jist ree-collect which. But he don't keep tavern on this road no more."

"Of course not," said his companion, "if he's a-livin' over the mountain. But I b'lieve he's dead."

I asked the other farmer if he knew how long it had been since Dutton had left this part of the country.

"I don't know fur certain," he said, "but I know he was keeping tavern here two year ago this fall, fur I came along here myself, an' stopped there to git supper—or dinner, I don't jist ree-collect which."

It had been three years since our friend had boarded at Dutton's house. There was no doubt that the man was not living at his old place. My wife and I now agreed that it was very foolish in us to come so far without making more particular inquiries. But we had had an idea that a man who had a place like Dutton's tavern would live there always.

"What are ye goin' to do?" asked the driver, very much interested, for it was not every day that he had passengers who had lost their destination. "Ye might go on to Lowry's. He takes boarders sometimes."

But Lowry's did not attract us. An ordinary country tavern, where stage-passengers took supper, was not what we came so far to find.

"Do you know where this house o' Dutton's is?" said the driver to the man who had once taken either dinner or supper there.

"Oh, yes! I'd know the house well enough, if I saw it. It's the fust house this side o' Lowry's."

"With a big pole in front of it?" asked the driver.

"Yes, there was a sign-pole in front of it."

"An' a long porch?"

"Yes."

"Oh, well!" said the driver, settling himself in his seat. "I know all about that house. That's a empty house. I didn't think you meant that house. There's nobody lives there. An' yit, now I come to remember, I have seen people about, too. I tell ye what ye better do. Since ye're so set on staying on this side the ridge, ye better let me put ye down at Dan Carson's place. That's jist about quarter of a mile from where Dutton used to live. Dan's wife can tell ye all about the Duttons, an' about everybody else, too, in this part o' the country, an' if there ain't nobody livin' at the old tavern, ye can stay all night at Carson's, an' I'll stop an' take you back to-morrow, when I come along."

We agreed to this plan, for there was nothing better to be done, and, late in the afternoon, we were set down with our small trunk—for we were travelling under light weight—at Dan Carson's door. The stage was rather behind time, and the driver whipped up and left us to settle our own affairs. He called back, however, that he would keep a good lookout for us to-morrow.

Mrs. Carson soon made her appearance, and, very naturally, was somewhat surprised to see visitors with their baggage standing on her little porch. She was a plain, coarsely dressed woman, with an apronful of chips and kindling-wood, and a fine mind for detail, as we soon discovered.

RUDDER GRANGE

"Jist so," said she, putting down the chips, and inviting us to seats on a bench. "Dave Dutton's folks is all moved away. Dave has a good farm on the other side o' the mountain, an' it never did pay him to keep that tavern, specially as he didn't sell liquor. When he went away, his son Al come there to live with his wife, an' the old man left a good deal o' furniter an' things fur him ; but Al's wife ain't satisfied here, an' though they've been here off an' on, the house is shet up most o' the time. It's fur sale an' to rent, both, ef anybody wants it. I'm sorry about you, too, fur it was a nice tavern when Dave kept it."

We admitted that we were also very sorry, and the kind-hearted woman showed a great deal of sympathy.

"You might stay here, but we hain't got no fit room where you two could sleep."

At this Euphemia and I looked very blank.

"But you could go up to the house an' stay, jist as well as not," Mrs. Carson continued. "There's plenty o' things there, an' I keep the key. For the matter o' that, ye might take the house for as long as ye want to stay ; Dave'd be glad enough to rent it, and if the lady knows how to keep house, it wouldn't be no trouble at all, jist for you two. We could let ye have all the victuals ye'd want, cheap, an' there's plenty o' wood there, cut, and everything handy."

We looked at each other. We agreed. Here was a chance for a rare good time. It might be better, perhaps, than anything we had expected.

The bargain was struck. Mrs. Carson, who seemed vested with all the necessary powers of attorney, appeared to be perfectly satisfied with our trust-worthiness, and when I paid on the spot the small sum she thought proper for two weeks' rent, she evidently considered she had done a very good thing for Dave Dutton and herself.

"I'll jist put some bread, an' eggs, an' coffee, an' pork, an' things in a basket, an' I'll have 'em took up fur ye, with yer trunk, an' I'll go with ye an' take some milk. Here, Danny!" she cried; and directly her husband, a long, thin, sunburnt, sandy-headed man, appeared, and to him she told, in a few words, our story, and ordered him to hitch up the cart and be ready to take our trunk and the basket up to Dutton's old house.

When all was ready, we walked up the hill, followed by Danny and the cart. We found the house a large, low, old-fashioned farm-house, standing near the road, with a long piazza in front, and a magnificent view of mountain-tops in the rear. Within, the lower rooms were large and low, with quite a good deal of furniture in them. There was no earthly reason why we should not be perfectly jolly and comfortable here. The more we saw, the more delighted we were at the odd experience we were about to have. Mrs. Carson busied herself in getting things in order for our supper and general accommodation. She made Danny carry our trunk to a bedroom in the second story, and then set him to work building a fire in a great fireplace with a crane for the kettle.

When she had done all she could it was nearly dark, and after lighting a couple of candles, she left us, to go home and get supper for her own family.

As she and Danny were about to depart in the cart, she ran back to ask us if we would like to borrow a dog.

205

" There ain't nothin' to be afeard of," she said, "for nobody hardly ever takes the trouble to lock the doors in these parts ; but bein' city folks, I thought ye might feel better if ye had a dog."

We made haste to tell her that we were not city folks, and declined the dog. Indeed, Euphemia remarked that she would be much more afraid of a strange dog than of robbers.

After supper, which we enjoyed as much as any meal we ever ate in our lives, we each took a candle, and after arranging our bedroom for the night, we explored the old house. There were lots of curious things everywhere—things that were apparently so "old-timey," as my wife remarked, that David Dutton did not care to take them with him to his new farm, and so left them for his son, who probably cared for them even less than his father did. There was a garret extending over the whole house, filled with old spinning-wheels, and strings of onions, and all sorts of antiquated bric-à-brac, which was so fascinating to me that I could scarcely tear myself away from it ; but Euphemia, who was dreadfully afraid that I would set the whole place on fire, at length prevailed on me to come down.

We slept soundly, that night, in what was probably the best bedroom of the house, and awoke with a feeling that we were about to enter on a period of some uncommon kind of jollity, which we found to be true when we went down to get breakfast. I made the fire, Euphemia made the coffee, and Mrs. Carson came with cream and some fresh eggs. The good woman was in high spirits. She was evidently pleased at the idea of having neighbors, temporary though they were, and it had probably been a long time since she had had such a chance of selling milk, eggs, and sundries. It was almost the same as opening a country store. We bought groceries and everything of her.

We had a glorious time that day. We were just starting out for a mountain stroll when our stage-driver came along on his down trip.

"Hello!" he called out. "Want to go back this morning?"

"Not a bit of it," I cried. "We won't go back for a couple of weeks. We've settled here for the present."

The man smiled. He didn't seem to understand it exactly, but he was evidently glad to see us so well satisfied. If he had had time to stop and have the matter explained to him, he would probably have been better satisfied; but, as it was, he waved his whip to us and drove on. He was a good fellow.

We strolled all day, having locked up the house and taken our lunch with us, and when we came back, it seemed really like coming home. Mrs. Carson, with whom we had left the key, had brought the milk and was making the fire. This woman was too kind. We determined to try to repay her in some way. After a splendid supper we went to bed happy.

The next day was a repetition of this one, but the day after it rained. So we determined to enjoy the old tavern, and we rummaged about everywhere. I visited the garret again, and we went to the old barn, with its mows half full of hay, and had rare times climbing about there. We were delighted that it happened to rain. In a woodshed, near the house, I saw a big square board with letters on it. I examined

the board, and found it was a sign,—a hanging sign,—
and on it was painted, in letters that were yet quite
plain :

FARMERS'

AND

MECHANICS'

HOTEL

I called to Euphemia and told her that I had found
the old tavern sign. She came to look at it, and I
pulled it out.

"'Soldiers and sailors'!" she exclaimed. "That's
funny."

I looked over on her side of the sign, and sure
enough, there was the inscription :

SOLDIERS'

AND

SAILORS'

HOUSE

"They must have bought this comprehensive sign
in some town," I said. "Such a name would never
have been chosen for a country tavern like this. But
I wish they hadn't taken it down. The house would
look more like what it ought to be with its sign hanging before it."

"Well, then," said Euphemia, "let's put it up."

I agreed instantly to this proposition, and we went
to look for a ladder. We found one in the wagon-
house, and carried it out to the sign-post in the front
of the house. It was raining gently during these performances, but we had on our old clothes, and were so
much interested in our work that we did not care for a

little rain. I carried the sign to the post, and then, at the imminent risk of breaking my neck, I hung it on its appropriate hooks on the transverse beam of the sign-post. Now our tavern was really what it pretended to be. We gazed on the sign with admiration and content.

"Do you think we would better keep it up all the time?" I asked of my wife.

"Certainly," said she. "It's a part of the house. The place isn't complete without it."

"But suppose some one should come along and want to be entertained?"

"But no one will. And if people do come, I'll take care of the soldiers and sailors, if you will attend to the farmers and mechanics."

I consented to this, and we went indoors to prepare dinner.

CHAPTER XVIII

OUR TAVERN

THE next day was clear again, and we rambled in the woods until the sun was nearly down, and so were late about supper. We were just taking our seats at the table when we heard a footstep on the front porch. Instantly the same thought came into each of our minds.

"I do believe," said Euphemia, "that's somebody who has mistaken this for a tavern. I wonder whether it's a soldier or a farmer or a sailor; but you would better go and see."

I went to see, prompted to move quickly by the newcomer pounding his cane on the bare floor of the hall. I found him standing just inside of the front door. He was a small man, with long hair and beard, and dressed in a suit of clothes of a remarkable color —something of the hue of faded snuff. He had a big stick, and carried a large, flat valise in one hand.

He bowed to me very politely.

"Can I stop here to-night?" he asked, taking off his hat as my wife put her head out of the kitchen door.

"Why—no, sir," I said. "This is not a tavern."

"Not a tavern!" he exclaimed. "I don't understand that. You have a sign out."

"That is true," I said, "but that is only for fun, so to speak. We are here temporarily, and we put up that sign just to please ourselves."

"That is pretty poor fun for me," said the man. "I am very tired, and more hungry than tired. Couldn't you let me have a little supper, at any rate?"

Euphemia glanced at me. I nodded.

"You are welcome to some supper," she said. "Come in! We eat in the kitchen because it is more convenient, and because it is so much more cheerful than the dining-room. There is a pump out there, and here is a towel, if you would like to wash your hands."

As the man went out the back door I complimented my wife. She was really an admirable hostess.

The individual in faded snuff-color was certainly hungry, and he seemed to enjoy his supper. During the meal he gave us some account of himself. He was an artist, and had travelled, mostly on foot, it would appear, over a great part of the country. He had in his valise some very pretty little colored sketches of scenes in Mexico and California, which he showed us after supper. Why he carried these pictures—which were done on stiff paper—about with him I do not know. He said he did not care to sell them, as he might use them for studies for larger pictures some day. His valise, which he opened wide on the table, seemed to be filled with papers, drawings, and matters of that kind. I suppose he preferred to wear his clothes, instead of carrying them about in his valise.

After sitting for about half an hour after supper, he rose, with an uncertain sort of smile, and said he supposed he must be moving on — asking, at the same time, how far it was to the tavern over the ridge.

"Just wait one moment, if you please," said Euphemia; and she beckoned me out of the room.

"Don't you think," said she, "that we could keep him all night? There's no moon, and it will be a fearfully dark walk, I know, to the other side of the mountain. There is a room up-stairs that I can make ready for him in ten minutes, and I know he's honest."

"How do you know it?" I asked.

"Well, because he wears such curious-colored clothes. No criminal would ever wear such clothes. He could never pass unnoticed anywhere; and being probably the only person in the world who dresses that way, he could always be detected."

"You are doubtless correct," I replied. "Let us keep him."

When we told the good man that he could stay all night, he was extremely obliged to us, and went to bed quite early. After we had fastened the house and had gone to our room, my wife said to me:

"Where is your pistol?"

I produced it.

"Well," said she, "I think you ought to have it where you can get at it."

"Why so?" I asked. "You generally want me to keep it out of sight and reach."

"Yes; but when there is a strange man in the house we ought to take extra precautions."

"But this man you say is honest," I replied. "If he committed a crime he could not escape—his appearance is so peculiar."

"But that wouldn't do us any good if we were both murdered," said Euphemia, pulling a chair up to my side of the bed, and laying the pistol carefully thereon, with the muzzle toward the bed.

We were not murdered, and we had a very pleasant breakfast with the artist, who told us more anecdotes of his life in Mexico and other places. When, after breakfast, he shut up his valise, preparatory to starting away, we felt really sorry. When he was ready to go, he asked for his bill.

"Oh! there is no bill," I exclaimed. "We have no idea of charging you anything. We don't really keep a hotel, as I told you."

"If I had known that," said he, looking very grave, "I would not have stayed. There is no reason why you should give me food and lodgings, and I would not, and did not, ask it. I am able to pay for such things, and I wish to do so."

We argued with him for some time, speaking of the habits of country people and so on, but he would not be convinced. He had asked for accommodation expecting to pay for it, and would not be content until he had done so.

"Well," said Euphemia, "we are not keeping this house for profit, and you can't force us to make anything out of you. If you will be satisfied to pay us just what it cost us to entertain you, I suppose we shall have to let you do that. Take a seat for a minute, and I will make out your bill."

So the artist and I sat down and talked of various matters, while my wife got out her travelling stationery box, and sat down to the dining-table to make out the bill. After a long, long time, as it appeared to me, I said:

"My dear, if the amount of that bill is at all pro-

RUDDER GRANGE

portioned to the length of time it takes to make it
out, I think our friend here will wish he had never
said anything about it."

"It's nearly done," said she, without raising her
head, and in about ten or fifteen minutes more she
rose and presented the bill to our guest. As I noticed
that he seemed somewhat surprised at it, I asked him
to let me look over it with him.

The bill, of which I have a copy, read as follows:

"July 12, 187-.

Artist,

To the S. and S. Hotel and F. and M. House.

To ⅛ one supper, July 11, which supper consisted of:

$\frac{1}{14}$ lb. coffee, at 35 cts.	2 ½ cts.
" " sugar, " 14 "	1 "
⅛ qt. milk, " 6 "	1 "
½ loaf bread " 6 "	3 "
⅛ lb. butter " 25 "	3⅛ "
½ " bacon " 25 "	12½ "
$\frac{1}{16}$ pk. potatoes at 60 cts. per bush.	$1\frac{14}{16}$ "
½ pt. hominy at 6 cts.	3 "

$27\frac{1}{16}$

⅓ of total . . . . . $09\frac{1}{48}$ cts.

To ⅓ one breakfast, July 12 (same as
above, with exception of eggs instead of
bacon, and with hominy omitted),

$24\frac{1}{16}$

⅓ total. . . . $08\frac{1}{48}$ "

To rent of one room and furniture, for one night,
in furnished house of fifteen rooms at $6.00 per
week for whole house . . . . $05\frac{2}{3}$ "

Amount due. . . . $22\frac{11}{24}$ cts."

214

RUDDER GRANGE

The worthy artist burst out laughing when he read
this bill, and so did I.

"You needn't laugh," said Euphemia, reddening a
little. "That is exactly what your entertainment
cost, and we do not intend to take a cent more. We
get things here in such small quantities that I can
tell quite easily what a meal costs us, and I have calculated that bill very carefully."

"So I should think, madam," said the artist, "but it
is not quite right. You have charged nothing for your
trouble and services."

"No," said my wife, "for I took no additional
trouble to get your meals. What I did, I should
have done if you had not come. To be sure, I did
spend a few minutes preparing your room. I will
charge you seven twenty-fourths of a cent for that,
thus making your bill twenty-three cents—even
money."

"I cannot gainsay reasoning like yours, madam,"
he said, and he took a quarter from a very fat old
pocket-book, and handed it to her. She gravely gave
him two cents change, and then, taking the bill, re-
ceipted it, and handed it back to him.

We were sorry to part with our guest, for he was
evidently a good fellow. I walked with him a little
way up the road, and got him to let me copy his bill
in my memorandum-book. The original, he said, he
would always keep.

A day or two after the artist's departure, we were
standing on the front piazza. We had had a late
breakfast,—consequent upon a long tramp the day
before,—and had come out to see what sort of a day it
was likely to be. We had hardly made up our minds

215

on the subject when the morning stage came up at full speed and stopped at our gate.

"Hello!" cried the driver. He was not our driver. He was a tall man in high boots, and had a great reputation as a manager of horses—so Danny Carson told me afterward. There were two drivers on the line, and each of them made one trip a day, going up one day in the afternoon, and down the next day in the morning.

I went out to see what this driver wanted.

"Can't you give my passengers breakfast?" he asked.

"Why, no!" I exclaimed, looking at the stage loaded inside and out. "This isn't a tavern. We couldn't get breakfast for a stage-load of people."

"What have you got a sign up fur, then?" roared the driver, getting red in the face.

"That's so," cried two or three men from the top of the stage. "If it ain't a tavern, what's that sign doin' there?"

I saw I must do something. I stepped up close to the stage, and looked in and up.

"Are there any sailors in this stage?" I said. There was no response. "Any soldiers? Any farmers or mechanics?"

At the latter question I trembled, but fortunately no one answered.

"Then," said I, "you have no right to ask to be accommodated; for, as you may see from the sign, our house is only for soldiers, sailors, farmers, and mechanics."

"And besides," cried Euphemia from the piazza, "we haven't anything to give you for breakfast."

216

The people in and on the stage grumbled a good deal at this, and looked as if they were both disappointed and hungry, while the driver ripped out an oath which, had he thrown it across a creek, would soon have made a good-sized mill-pond.

He gathered up his reins and turned a sinister look on me.

"I'll be even with you yit!" he cried as he dashed off.

In the afternoon Mrs. Carson came up and told us that the stage had stopped there, and that she had managed to give the passengers some coffee, bread and butter, and ham and eggs, though they had had to wait their turns for cups and plates. It appeared that the driver had quarrelled with the Lowry people that morning because the breakfast was behindhand and he was kept waiting. So he told his passengers that there was another tavern a few miles down the road, and that he would take them there to breakfast.

"He's an awful ugly man, that he is," said Mrs. Carson, "an' he'd better 'a' stayed at Lowry's, fur he had to wait a good sight longer, after all, as it turned out. But he's dreadful mad at you, an' says he'll bring ye farmers, an' soldiers, an' sailors, an' mechanics, if that's what ye want. I 'spect he'll do his best to git a load of them particular people an' drop 'em at yer door. I'd take down that sign, ef I was you. Not that me an' Danny minds, fur we're glad to git a stage to feed; an' ef you've any single man that wants lodgin', we've fixed up a room an' kin keep him overnight."

Notwithstanding this warning, Euphemia and I decided not to take in our sign. We were not to be

217

frightened by a stage-driver. The next day our own
driver passed us on the road as he was going down.

"So ye're pertickler about the people ye take in,
are ye?" said he, smiling. "That's all right, but ye
made Bill awful mad."

It was quite late on a Monday afternoon that Bill
stopped at our house again. He did not call out this
time. He simply drew up, and a man with a big
black valise clambered down from the top of the stage.
Then Bill shouted to me, as I walked down to the gate,
looking rather angry, I suppose:

"I was a-goin' to git ye a whole stage-load to stay
all night, but that one'll do ye, I reckon. Ha, ha!"
And off he went, probably fearing that I would throw
his passenger up on the top of the stage again.

The newcomer entered the gate. He was a dark
man, with black hair and black whiskers and mus-
tache, and black eyes. He wore clothes that had been
black, but which were now toned down by a good
deal of dust, and, as I have said, he carried a black
valise.

"Why did you stop here?" said I, rather inhospi-
tably. "Don't you know that we do not accommodate—"

"Yes, I know," he said, walking up on the piazza
and setting down his valise, "that you only take soldiers, sailors, farmers, and mechanics at this house. I
have been told all about it, and if I had not thoroughly
understood the matter I should not have thought of
such a thing as stopping here. If you will sit down
for a few moments I will explain." Saying this, he
took a seat on a bench by the door; but Euphemia
and I continued to stand.

RUDDER GRANGE

"I am," he continued, "a soldier, a sailor, a farmer, and a mechanic. Do not doubt my word; I will prove it to you in two minutes. When but seventeen years of age, circumstances compelled me to take charge of a farm in New Hampshire, and I kept up that farm until I was twenty-five. During this time I built several barns, wagon-houses, and edifices of that sort on my place, and becoming expert in this branch of mechanical art, I was much sought after by the neighboring farmers, who employed me to do similar work for them. In time I found this new business so profitable that I gave up farming altogether. But certain unfortunate speculations threw me on my back, and finally, having gone from bad to worse, I found myself in Boston, where, in sheer desperation, I went on board a coasting vessel as landsman. I remained on this vessel for nearly a year, but it did not suit me. I was often sick, and did not like the work. I left the vessel at one of the Southern ports, and it was not long after she sailed that, finding myself utterly without means, I enlisted as a soldier. I remained in the army for some years, and was finally honorably discharged. So you see that what I said was true. I belong to each and all of these businesses and professions. And now that I have satisfied you on this point, let me show you a book for which I have the agency in this country." He stooped down, opened his valise, and took out a good-sized volume. "This book," said he, "is the 'Flora and Fauna of Carthage County;' it is written by one of the first scientific men of the country, and gives you a description, with an authentic woodcut, of each of the plants and animals of the county—indigenous or naturalized. Owing

219

to peculiar advantages enjoyed by our firm, we are enabled to put this book at the very low price of three dollars and seventy-five cents. It is sold by subscription only, and should be on the centre-table in every parlor in this county. If you will glance over this book, sir, you will find it as interesting as a novel and as useful as an encyclopædia—"

"I don't want the book," I said, "and I don't care to look at it."

"But if you were to look at it you would want it, I'm sure."

"That's a good reason for not looking at it, then," I answered. "If you came to get us to subscribe for that book, we need not take up any more of your time, for we shall not subscribe."

"Oh, I did not come for that alone," he said. "I shall stay here to-night, and start out in the morning to work up the neighborhood. If you would like this book,—and I'm sure you have only to look at it to do that,—you can deduct the amount of my bill from the subscription price, and—"

"What did you say you charge for this book?" asked Euphemia, stepping forward and picking up the volume.

"Three seventy-five is the subscription price, ma'am. But that book is not for sale. That is merely a sample. If you put your name down on my list you will be served with your book in two weeks. As I told your husband, it will come very cheap to you, because you can deduct what you charge me for supper, lodging, and breakfast."

"Indeed!" said my wife; and then she remarked that she must go in the house and get supper.

RUDDER GRANGE

"When will supper be ready?" the man asked, as she passed him.

At first she did not answer him, but then she called back:

"In about half an hour."

"Good," said the man; "but I wish it was ready now. And now, sir, if you would just glance over this book while we are waiting for supper—"

I cut him very short, and went out into the road. I walked up and down in front of the house, in a bad humor. I could not bear to think of my wife getting supper for this fellow, who was striding about on the piazza as if he was very hungry and very impatient. Just as I returned to the house, the bell rang from within.

"Joyful sound!" said the man, and in he marched. I followed close behind him. On one end of the table, in the kitchen, supper was set for one person, and, as the man entered, Euphemia motioned him to the table. The supper looked like a remarkably good one. A cup of coffee smoked by the side of the plate; there was broiled ham and a small omelet; there were fried potatoes, some fresh radishes, a plate of hot biscuit, and some preserves. The man's eyes sparkled.

"I am sorry," said he, "that I am to eat alone, for I hoped to have your good company, but if this plan suits you, it suits me;" and he drew up a chair.

"Stop!" said Euphemia, advancing between him and the table. "You are not to eat that. That is a sample supper. If you order a supper like it, one will be served to you in two weeks."

At this I burst into a roar of laughter. My wife

221

stood pale and determined, and the man drew back, looking first at one of us, and then at the other.

"Am I to understand—?" he said.

"Yes," I interrupted, "you are. There is nothing more to be said on this subject. You may go now. You came here to annoy us, knowing that we did not entertain travellers, and now you see what you have made by it;" and I opened the door.

The man evidently thought that a reply was not necessary, and he walked out without a word. Taking up his valise, which he had put in the hall, he asked if there was any public house near by.

"No," I said, "but there is a farm-house, a short distance down the road, where they will be glad to have you." Down the road he went to Mrs. Carson's. I am sorry to say that he sold her a "Flora and Fauna" before he went to bed that night.

We were much amused at the termination of this affair, and I became, if possible, a still greater admirer of Euphemia's talents for management. But we both agreed that it would not do to keep up the sign any longer. We could not tell when the irate driver might not pounce down upon us with a customer.

"But I hate to take it down," said Euphemia, "it looks so much like a surrender."

"Do not trouble yourself," said I. "I have an idea."

The next morning I went down to Danny Carson's little shop,—he was a wheelwright as well as a farmer, and I got from him two pots of paint, one black and one white, and some brushes. I took down our sign, and painted out the old lettering, and, instead of it, I painted, in bold and somewhat regular characters, new names for our tavern.

RUDDER GRANGE

On one side of the sign I painted :

SOAP-MAKERS'

AND

BOOKBINDERS'

HOTEL

And on the other side :

UPHOLSTERERS'

AND

DENTISTS'

HOUSE

"Now, then," I said, "I don't believe any of those people will be travelling along the road while we are here, or, at any rate, they won't want to stop."

We admired this sign very much, and sat on the piazza that afternoon to see how it would strike Bill as he passed by. It seemed to strike him pretty hard, for he gazed with all his eyes at one side of it as he approached, and then, as he passed it, he actually pulled up to read the other side.

"All right!" he called out, as he drove off. "All right! All right!"

Euphemia didn't like the way he said "all right." It seemed to her, she said, as if he intended to do something which would be all right for him, but not at all for us. I saw she was nervous about it, for that evening she began to ask me questions about the travelling propensities of soap-makers, upholsterers, and dentists.

"Do not think anything more about that, my dear," I said. "I will take the sign down in the morning. We are here to enjoy ourselves, and not to be worried."

"And yet," said she, "it would worry me to think that that driver frightened us into taking down the

223

sign. I tell you what I wish you would do. Paint out those names, and let me make a sign. Then I promise you I shall not be worried."

The next day, therefore, I took down the sign and painted out my inscriptions. It was a good deal of trouble, for my letters were fresh; but as it was a rainy day, I had plenty of time, and succeeded tolerably well. Then I gave Euphemia the black-paint pot and the freedom of the sign.

I went down to the creek to try a little fishing in wet weather, and when I returned the new sign was done. On one side it read:

FLIES'
AND
WASPS'
HOTEL

On the other:

HUNDRED-LEGGERS'
AND
RED-ANTS'
HOUSE

"You see," said Euphemia, "if any individuals mentioned thereon apply for accommodation, we can say we are full." This sign hung triumphantly for several days, when, one morning, just as we had finished breakfast, we were surprised to hear the stage stop at the door, and before we could go out to see who had arrived, into the room came our own stage-driver, as we used to call him. He had actually left his team to come to see us.

"I just thought I'd stop an' tell ye," said he, "that ef ye don't look out, Bill 'll get ye inter trouble. He's bound to git the best o' ye, an' I heared this mornin', at Lowry's, that he's a-goin' to bring the county clerk up here to-morrow, to see about yer license fur keepin' a hotel. He says ye keep changin' yer signs, but that don't differ to him, for he kin prove ye've kept travellers overnight, an' ef ye haven't got no license he'll make the county clerk come down on ye heavy, I'm sure o' that, fur I know Bill. An' so, I thought I'd stop an' tell ye."

I thanked him, and admitted that this was a rather serious view of the case. Euphemia pondered a moment. Then said she :

"I don't see why we should stay here any longer. It's going to rain again, and our vacation is up to-morrow, anyway. Could you wait a short time, while we pack up ? " she said to the driver.

"Oh, yes ! " he replied. "I kin wait, as well as not. I've only got one passenger, an' he's on top, a-holdin' the horses. He ain't in any hurry, I know, an' I'm ahead o' time."

In less than twenty minutes we had packed our trunk, locked up the house, and were in the stage ; as we drove away we cast a last admiring look at Euphemia's sign, slowly swinging in the wind. I would much like to know if it is swinging there yet. I feel certain there has been no lack of custom.

We stopped at Mrs. Carson's, paid her what we owed her, and engaged her to go up to the tavern and put things in order. She was very sorry we were going, but hoped we would come back again some other summer. We said that it was quite possible that we might do so, but that next time we did not think we would try to have a tavern of our own.

CHAPTER XIX

THE BABY AT RUDDER GRANGE

For some reason, not altogether understood by me, there seemed to be a continued series of new developments at our home. I had supposed, when the events spoken of in the last chapter had settled down to their proper places in our little history, that our life would flow on in an even, commonplace way, with few or no incidents worthy of being recorded. But this did not prove to be the case. After a time, the uniformity and quiet of our existence was considerably disturbed.

This disturbance was caused by a baby; not a rude, imperious baby, but a child who was generally of a quiet and orderly turn of mind. But it disarranged all our plans, all our habits, all the ordinary disposition of things.

It was in the summer-time, during my vacation, that it began to exert its full influence upon us. A more unfortunate season could not have been selected. At first I may say that it did not exert its full influence upon me. I was away during the day, and in the evening its influence was not exerted to any great extent upon anybody. As I have said, its habits were exceedingly orderly. But during my vacation the things came to pass which have made this chapter necessary.

I did not intend taking a trip. As in a former vacation, I proposed staying at home and enjoying those delights of the country which my business in town did not allow me to enjoy in the working weeks and months of the year. I had no intention of camping out, or of doing anything of that kind, but many were the trips, rides, and excursions I had planned.

I found, however, that if I enjoyed myself in this wise, I must do it, for the most part, alone. It was not that Euphemia could not go with me—there was really nothing to prevent; it was simply that she had lost, for the time, her interest in everything except that baby.

She wanted me to be happy, to amuse myself, to take exercise, to do whatever I thought was pleasant; but she herself was so much engrossed with the child that she was often ignorant of what I intended to do, or had done. She thought she was listening to what I said to her, but in reality she was occupied, mind and body, with the baby, or listening for some sound which should indicate that she ought to go and be occupied with it.

I would often say to her: "Why can't you let Pomona attend to it? You surely need not give up your whole time and your whole mind to the child."

But she would always answer that Pomona had a great many things to do, and that she couldn't at all times attend to the baby. Suppose, for instance, that she should be at the barn.

I once suggested that a nurse should be procured, but at this she laughed.

"There is very little to do," she said, "and I really like to do it."

"Yes," said I, "but you spend so much of your time in thinking how glad you will be to do that little, when it is to be done, that you can't give me any attention at all."

"Now, you have no cause to say that," she exclaimed. "You know very well—there!" and away she ran. It had just begun to cry!

Naturally, I was getting tired of this. I could never begin a sentence and feel sure that I would be allowed to finish it. Nothing was important enough to delay attention to an infantile whimper.

Jonas, too, was in a state of unrest. He was obliged to wear his good clothes a great part of the time, for he was continually going on errands to the village, and these errands were so important that they took precedence of everything else. It gave me a melancholy sort of pleasure, sometimes, to do Jonas's work when he was thus sent away.

I asked him, one day, how he liked it all?

"Well," said he, reflectively, "I can't say as I understand it, exactly. It does seem queer to me that such a little thing should take up pretty nigh all the time of three people. I suppose, after a while,"—this he said with a grave smile,—"that you may be wanting to turn in and help." I did not make any answer to this, for Jonas was, at that moment, summoned to the house ; but it gave me an idea—in fact, it gave me two ideas.

The first was that Jonas's remark was not entirely respectful. He was my hired man, but he was very respectable, and an American, and therefore might sometimes be expected to say things which a foreigner, not known to be respectable, would not think of saying, if he wished to keep his place. The fact that Jonas had always been very careful to treat me with much civility caused this remark to make more impression on me. I felt that he had, in a measure, reason for it.

The other idea was one which grew and developed in my mind until I afterward formed a plan upon it. I determined, however, before I carried out my plan, to again try to reason with Euphemia.

"If it was our own baby," I said, "or even the child of one of us by a former marriage, it would be a different thing, but to give yourself up so entirely to Pomona's baby seems to me unreasonable. Indeed, I never heard of any case exactly like it. It is reversing all the usages of society for the mistress to take care of the servant's baby."

"The usages of society are not worth much, sometimes," said Euphemia, "and you must remember that Pomona is a very different kind of a person from an ordinary servant. She is much more like a member of the family—I can't exactly explain what kind of a member, but I understand it myself. She has very much improved since she has been married, and you know yourself how quiet and—and nice she is; and as for the baby, it's just as good and pretty as any baby, and it may grow up to be better than any of us. Some of our Presidents have sprung from lowly parents."

"But this baby is a girl," I said.

"Well, then," replied Euphemia, "she may be a President's wife."

"Another thing," I remarked; "I don't believe Jonas and Pomona like your keeping their baby so much to yourself."

"Nonsense!" said Euphemia. "A girl in Pomona's position couldn't help being glad to have a lady take an interest in her baby, and help bring it up. And as for Jonas, he would be a cruel man if he weren't pleased and grateful to have his wife relieved of so much trouble. Pomona! is that you? You can bring it here now, if you want to get at your clear-starching."

I do not believe that Pomona hankered after clear-starching, but she brought the baby, and I went away. I could not see any hope ahead. Of course, in time it would grow up; but then, it couldn't grow up during my vacation.

Then it was that I determined to carry out my plan.

I went to the stable and harnessed the horse to the little carriage. Jonas was not there, and I had fallen out of the habit of calling him. I drove slowly through the yard and out of the gate. No one called to me or asked where I was going. How different this was from the old times! Then some one would not have failed to know where I was going, and, in all probability, she would have gone with me. But now I drove away quietly and undisturbed.

About three miles from our house was a settlement known as New Dublin. It was a cluster of poor and doleful houses, inhabited entirely by Irish people, whose dirt and poverty seemed to make them very contented and happy. The men were generally away at their work during the day, but there was never any difficulty in finding some one at home, no matter

at what house one called. I was acquainted with one
of the matrons of this locality, a Mrs. Duffy, who had
occasionally undertaken some odd jobs at our house,
and to her I made a visit.

She was glad to see me, and wiped off a chair for me.

"Mrs. Duffy," said I, "I want to rent a baby."

At first the good woman could not understand me;
but when I made plain to her that I wished, for a short
time, to obtain the exclusive use and control of a baby,
for which I was willing to pay a liberal rental, she
burst into long and violent laughter. It seemed to
her like a person coming into the country to purchase
weeds. Weeds and children were so abundant in New
Dublin. But she gradually began to see that I was
in earnest, and as she knew I was a trusty person,
and somewhat noted for the care I took of my live
stock, she was perfectly willing to accommodate me,
but feared she had nothing on hand of the age I
desired.

"Me childther are all a-goin' about," she said. "Ye
kin see a poile uv 'em out yon in the road, an' there's
more uv 'em on the fince. But ye nade have no fear
about gittin' wan. There's sthacks of 'em in the place.
I'll jist run over to Mrs. Hogan's wid ye. She's got
sixteen or siventeen, mostly small, for Hogan brought
four or five wid him when he married her, an' she'll
be glad to rint wan uv 'em." So, throwing her apron
over her head, she accompanied me to Mrs. Hogan's.

That lady was washing, but she cheerfully stopped
her work while Mrs. Duffy took her to one side and
explained my errand. Mrs. Hogan did not appear to
be able to understand why I wanted a baby,—especially
for so limited a period,—but probably concluded that

231

if I would take good care of it and would pay well for it, the matter was my own affair, for she soon came and said that if I wanted a baby I'd come to the right place. Then she began to consider what one she would let me have. I insisted on a young one—there was already a little baby at our house, and the folks there would know how to manage it.

"Oh, ye want it fur coompany for the ither one, is that it?" said Mrs. Hogan, a new light breaking in upon her. "An' that's a good plan, sure. It must be dridful lownly in a house wid ownly wan baby. Now, there's one—Polly—would she do?"

"Why, she can run," I said. "I don't want one that can run."

"Oh, dear!" said Mrs. Hogan, with a sigh, "they all begin to run very airly. Now, Polly isn't owld at all, at all."

"I can see that," said I, "but I want one that you can put in a cradle—one that will have to stay there when you put it in."

It was plain that Mrs. Hogan's present stock did not contain exactly what I wanted, and directly Mrs. Duffy exclaimed : "There's Mary McCann—an' roight across the way!"

Mrs. Hogan said, "Yis, sure," and we all went over to a little house opposite.

"Now, thin," said Mrs. Duffy, entering the house, and proudly drawing a small coverlet from a little box-bed in a corner, "what do you think of that?"

"Why, there are two of them!" I exclaimed.

"To be sure," said Mrs. Duffy. "They're tweens. There's always two uv 'em when they're tweens. An' they're young enough."

"They're tweens."

RUDDER GRANGE

"Yes," said I, doubtfully, "but I couldn't take both. Do you think their mother would rent one of them?"

The women shook their heads. "Ye see, sir," said Mrs. Hogan, "Mary McCann isn't here, bein' gone out to a wash, but she ownly has four or foive childther, an' she ain't much used to 'em yit, an' I kin spake fur her that she'd niver siparate a pair o' tweens. When she gits a dozen hersilf, and marries a widow gintleman wid a lot uv his own, she'll be glad enough to be lettin' ye have yer pick, to take wan uv 'em fur coompany to yer own baby, at foive dollars a week. Moind that."

I visited several houses after this, still in company with Mrs. Hogan and Mrs. Duffy, and finally secured a youngish infant, who, having been left motherless, had become what Mrs. Duffy called a "bottle-baby," and was in charge of a neighboring aunt. It seemed strange that this child, so eminently adapted to purposes of rental, was not offered to me at first, but I suppose the Irish ladies who had the matter in charge wanted to benefit themselves, or some of their near friends, before giving the general public of New Dublin a chance.

The child suited me very well, and I agreed to take it for as many days as I might happen to want it, but to pay by the week, in advance. It was a boy, with a suggestion of orange-red bloom all over its head, and what looked to me like freckles on its cheeks; while its little nose turned up—even more than those of babies generally turn—above a very long upper lip. His eyes were blue and twinkling, and he had the very mouth "fur a leetle poipe," as Mrs. Hogan admiringly remarked.

233

He was hastily prepared for his trip, and when I had arranged the necessary business matters with his aunt, and had assured her that she could come to see him whenever she liked, I got into the carriage, and having spread the lap-robe over my knees, the baby, carefully wrapped in a little shawl, was laid in my lap. Then his bottle, freshly filled, for he might need a drink on the way, was tucked between the cushions on the seat beside me, and taking the lines in my left hand, while I steadied my charge with the other, I prepared to drive away.

"What's his name?" I asked.

"It's Pat," said his aunt, "afther his dad, who's away in the moines."

"But ye kin call him onything ye loike," Mrs. Duffy remarked, "fur he don't ansther to his name yit."

"Pat will do very well," I said, as I bade the good women farewell, and carefully guided the horse through the swarm of youngsters who had gathered around the carriage.

CHAPTER XX

I DROVE slowly home, and little Pat lay very quiet, looking up steadily at me with his twinkling blue eyes. For a time everything went very well; but happening to look up, I saw in the distance a carriage approaching. It was an open barouche, and I knew it belonged to a family of our acquaintance in the village, and that it usually contained ladies.

Quick as thought, I rolled up Pat in his shawl and stuffed him under the seat. Then, rearranging the lap-robe over my knees, I drove on, trembling a little, it is true.

As I supposed, the carriage contained ladies, and I knew them all. The coachman instinctively drew up as we approached. We always stopped and spoke on such occasions.

They asked me after my wife, apparently surprised to see me alone, and made a number of pleasant observations, to all of which I replied with as unconcerned and easy an air as I could assume. The ladies were in excellent spirits, but in spite of this there seemed to be an air of repression about them, which I thought of when I drove on, but could not account for, for little Pat never moved or whimpered during the whole of the interview.

But when I took him again in my lap, and happened to turn as I arranged the robe, I saw his bottle sticking up boldly by my side from between the cushions. Then I did not wonder at the repression.

When I reached home, I drove directly to the barn. Fortunately, Jonas was there. When I called him and handed little Pat to him I never saw a man more utterly amazed. He stood and held the child without a word. But when I explained the whole affair to him, he comprehended it perfectly, and was delighted. I think he was just as anxious for my plan to work as I was myself, although he did not say so.

I was about to take the child into the house, when Jonas remarked that it was barefooted.

"That won't do," I said. "It certainly had socks on when I got it. I saw them."

"Here they are," said Jonas, fishing them out from the shawl; "he's kicked them off."

"Well, we must put them on," I said; "it won't do to take him in that way. You hold him."

So Jonas sat down on the feed-box, and carefully taking little Pat, he held him horizontally, firmly pressed between his hands and knees, with his feet stuck out toward me, while I knelt down before him and tried to put on the little socks. But the socks were knit or worked very loosely, and there seemed to be a good many small holes in them, so that Pat's funny little toes, which he kept curling up and un-curling, were continually making their appearance in unexpected places through the sock. But, after a great deal of trouble, I got them both on, with the heels in about the right places.

"Now they ought to be tied on," I said. "Where are his garters?"

"I don't believe babies have garters," said Jonas, doubtfully, "but I could rig him up a pair."

"No," said I, "we won't take the time for that. I'll hold his legs apart as I carry him in. It's rubbing his feet together that gets them off."

As I passed the kitchen window I saw Pomona at work. She looked at me, dropped something, and I heard a crash. I don't know how much that crash cost me. Jonas rushed in to tell Pomona about it, and in a moment I heard a scream of laughter. At this, Euphemia appeared at an upper window, with her hand raised, and saying severely : "Hush-h !" But the moment she saw me, she disappeared from the window and came down-stairs on the run. She met me just as I entered the dining-room.

"What *in* the world !" she breathlessly exclaimed.

"This," said I, taking Pat into a better position in my arms, "is my baby."

"Your—baby !" said Euphemia. "Where did you get it? What are you going to do with it?"

"I got it in New Dublin," I replied, "and I want it to amuse and occupy me while I am at home. I haven't anything else to do, except things that take me away from you."

"Oh !" said Euphemia.

At this moment little Pat gave his first whimper. Perhaps he felt the searching glance that fell upon him from the lady in the middle of the room.

I immediately began to walk up and down the floor with him, and to sing to him. I did not know any infant music, but I felt sure that a soothing tune was

237

the great requisite, and that the words were of small importance. So I started on an old Methodist tune, which I remembered very well, and which was used with the hymn containing the line,

"Weak and wounded, sick and sore,"

and I sang, as soothingly as I could:

> "Lit-tle Pat-sy, Wat-sy, Sat-sy,
> Does he feel a lit-ty bad?
> Me will send and get his bot-tle;
> He sha'n't have to cry-wy-wy."

"What an idiot!" said Euphemia, laughing in spite of her vexation.

> "No, we ain't no id-i-otses;
> What we want's a bot-ty mi'k."

So I sang as I walked to the kitchen door and sent Jonas to the barn for the bottle.

Pomona was in spasms of laughter in the kitchen, and Euphemia was trying her best not to laugh at all.

"Who's going to take care of it, I'd like to know?" she said, as soon as she could get herself into a state of severe inquiry.

> "Some-times me, and some-times Jonas,"

I sang, still walking up and down the room with a long, slow step, swinging the baby from side to side, very much as if it were grass-seed in a sieve, and I were sowing it over the carpet.

When the bottle came, I took it, and began to feed little Pat. Perhaps the presence of a critical and interested audience embarrassed us,—for Jonas and

Pomona were at the door, with streaming eyes, while Euphemia stood with her handkerchief to the lower part of her face,—or it may have been that I did not understand the management of bottles, but, at any rate, I could not make the thing work, and the disappointed little Pat began to cry, just as the whole of our audience burst into a wild roar of laughter.

"Here! Give me that child!" cried Euphemia, forcibly taking Pat and the bottle from me. "You'll make it swallow the whole affair, and I'm sure its mouth's big enough."

"You really don't think," she said, when we were alone, and little Pat, with his upturned blue eyes serenely surveying the features of the good lady who knew how to feed him, was placidly pulling away at his india-rubber tube, "that I will consent to your keeping such a creature as this in the house? Why, he's a regular little Paddy! If you kept him he'd grow up into a hod-carrier."

"Good!" said I. "I never thought of that. What a novel thing it would be to witness the gradual growth of a hod-carrier! I'll make him a little hod now, to begin with. He couldn't have a more suitable toy."

"I was talking in earnest," she said. "Take your baby, and please carry him home as quick as you can, for I am certainly not going to take care of him."

"Of course not," said I. "Now that I see how it's done, I'm going to do it myself. Jonas will mix his feed and I will give it to him. He looks sleepy now. Shall I take him up-stairs and lay him on our bed?"

"No, indeed," cried Euphemia. "You can put him on a quilt on the floor until after luncheon, and then you must take him home."

I laid the young Milesian on the folded quilt which Euphemia prepared for him, where he turned up his little pug nose to the ceiling and went contentedly to sleep.

That afternoon I nailed four legs on a small packing-box and made a bedstead for him. This, with a pillow in the bottom of it, was very comfortable, and instead of taking him home, I borrowed, in the evening, some baby night-clothes from Pomona, and set about preparing Pat for the night.

This Euphemia would not allow, but silently taking him from me, she put him to bed.

"To-morrow," she said, "you must positively take him away. I won't stand it. And in our room, too."

"I didn't talk in that way about the baby you adopted," I said.

To this she made no answer, but went away to attend, as usual, to Pomona's baby, while its mother washed the dishes.

That night little Pat woke up, several times, and made things unpleasant by his wails. On the first two occasions, I got up and walked him about, singing impromptu lines to the tune of "weak and wounded;" but the third time, Euphemia herself arose, and, declaring that that doleful tune was a great deal worse than the baby's crying, silenced him herself, arranging his couch more comfortably, and he troubled us no more.

In the morning, when I beheld the little pad of orange fur in the box, my heart almost misgave me; but as the day wore on my courage rose again, and I gave myself up, almost entirely, to my new charge, composing a vast deal of blank verse while walking him up and down the house.

Euphemia scolded and scolded, and said she would put on her hat and go for the mother. But I told her the mother was dead, and that seemed to be an obstacle. She took a good deal of care of the child, for she said she would not see an innocent creature neglected, even if it were an incipient hod-carrier, but she did not relax in the least her attention to Pomona's baby.

The next day was about the same in regard to infantile incident; but on the day after I began to tire of my new charge, and Pat, on his side, seemed to be tired of me, for he turned from me when I went to take him up, while he held out his hands to Euphemia, and grinned delightedly when she took him.

That morning I drove to the village and spent an hour or two there. On my return I found Euphemia sitting in our room, with little Pat on her lap. I was astonished at the change in the young rascal. He was dressed, from head to foot, in a suit of clothes belonging to Pomona's baby; the glowing fuzz on his head was brushed and made as smooth as possible, while his little muslin sleeves were tied up with blue ribbon.

I stood speechless at the sight.

"Doesn't he look nice?" said Euphemia, standing him up on her knees. "It shows what good clothes will do. I'm glad I helped Pomona make up so many. He's getting ever so fond of me—ze itty Patsy, watsy! See how strong he is! He can almost stand on his legs! Look how he laughs! He's just as cunning as he can be. And oh! I was going to speak about that box. I wouldn't have him sleep in that old packing-box. There are little wicker cradles at the store— I saw them last week; they don't cost much, and you could bring one up in the carriage. There's the other baby crying, and I don't know where Pomona is. Just you mind him a minute, please!" And out she ran.

I looked out of the window. The horse still stood harnessed to the carriage, as I had left him. I saw Pat's old shawl lying in a corner. I seized it, and rolling him in it, new clothes and all, I hurried downstairs, climbed into the carriage, hastily disposed Pat in my lap, and turned the horse. The demeanor of the youngster was very different from what it was when I first took him in my lap to drive away with him. There was no confiding twinkle in his eye, no contented munching of his little fists. He gazed up at me with wild alarm, and as I drove out of the gate he burst forth into such a yell that Lord Edward came bounding around the house to see what was the matter. Euphemia suddenly appeared at an upper window and called out to me, but I did not hear what she said. I whipped up the horse, and we sped along to New Dublin. Pat soon stopped crying, but he looked at me with a tear-stained and reproachful visage.

The good women of the settlement were surprised to see little Pat return so soon.

"An' wasn't he good?" said Mrs. Hogan, as she took him from my hands.

"Oh, yes!" I said. "He was as good as he could be. But I have no further need of him."

I might have been called upon to explain this statement, had not the whole party of women who stood around burst into wild expressions of delight at Pat's beautiful clothes.

"Oh! jist look at 'em!" cried Mrs. Duffy. "An' see thim leetle pittycoots, thrimmed wid lace! Oh, an' it was good in ye, sir, to give him all thim, an' pay the foive dollars, too."

"An' I'm glad he's back," said the fostering aunt, "for I was a-coomin' over to till ye that I've been hearin' from ould Pat, his dad, an' he's a-coomin' back from the moines, an' I don't know what he'd 'a' said if he'd found his leetle Pat was rinted. But if ye iver want to borry him, for a whoile, after ould Pat's gone back, ye kin have him rint-free ; an' it's much obloiged I am to ye, sir, fur dressin' him so foine."

I made no encouraging remarks as to future transactions in this line, and drove slowly home.

Euphemia met me at the door. She had Pomona's baby in her arms. We walked together into the parlor.

"And so you have given up the little fellow that you were going to do so much for ? " she said.

"Yes, I have given him up," I answered.

"It must have been a dreadful trial to you," she continued.

"Oh, dreadful !" I replied.

"I suppose you thought he would take up so much of your time and thoughts that we couldn't be to each other what we used to be, didn't you ? " she said.

"Not exactly," I replied. "I only thought that things promised to be twice as bad as they were before."

She made no answer to this, but going to the back door of the parlor, she opened it and called Pomona. When that young woman appeared, Euphemia stepped toward her and said : "Here, Pomona, take your baby."

They were simple words, but they were spoken in such a way that they meant a good deal. Pomona knew what they meant. Her eyes sparkled, and as she went out, I saw her hug her child to her breast and cover it with kisses, and then, through the window, I could see her running to the barn and Jonas.

"Now, then," said Euphemia, closing the door and coming toward me with one of her old smiles, and not a trace of preoccupation about her, "I suppose you expect me to devote myself to you."

I did expect it, and I was not mistaken.

www.ingramcontent.com/pod-product-compliance
Lightning Source LLC
Chambersburg PA
CBHW020614260626
47157CB00003B/1002